caillou®

The Wolf

Text: Joceline Sanschagrin • Illustrations: Claude Lapierre

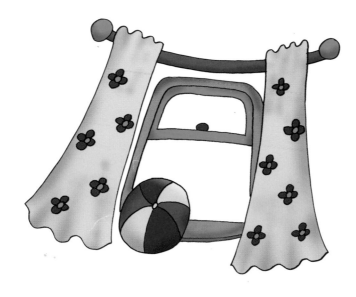

chouette

Caillou watched Daddy come down
from the attic. Caillou was very curious.
He had never been up there.
Caillou decided to go into the attic too.

Caillou climbed the stairs.
It was dark in the attic and very quiet.
Caillou was scared. He thought
he saw a wolf in the shadows.

Caillou ran back downstairs.
He was out of breath and his heart
was pounding.
"Daddy, there's a wolf in the attic,"
he shouted.

Daddy looked surprised.
"A wolf? Are you sure, Caillou?
I've never seen a wolf in the attic.
Tell me what you saw."
"I saw a wolf with big teeth
and big ears," said Caillou.

"The wolf you saw must be really big,
Caillou," said Daddy.
"His eyes were red like fire,"
Caillou continued.
Daddy listened carefully.
"You must have been scared, Caillou.
Tell me again what happened."

Caillou wanted to talk about
the wolf he saw.
He told Daddy what the wolf was doing.
"The wolf was prowling around and
it was puffing and growling."
Caillou imitated the sound of the wolf.
He walked on tiptoe, huffing and puffing.

Caillou wasn't as scared when
he told Daddy about the wolf.
"The wolf had long fur and smelled bad,"
he said. "It looked very mean.
I'm going to catch it and throw it
out the window!"

Daddy took Caillou by the hand.
"Come with me, Caillou.
We've got to find this wolf.
Let's go to the attic together."
Caillou was worried.
He held Daddy's hand tightly as
they climbed the stairs.

Caillou and Daddy looked all
around the attic. "No..., no wolf
here...," said Daddy. "No wolf
there..., or there..."
Caillou and Daddy searched the entire attic.
They didn't find any sign of a wolf.

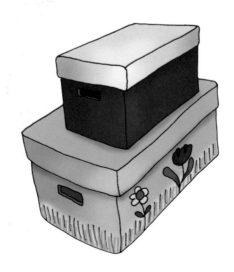

"Well, Caillou, where's the wolf?"
asked Daddy.
"I don't see it," Caillou replied.
Then Daddy explained,
"You were very scared, Caillou.
Maybe you thought you saw a wolf."

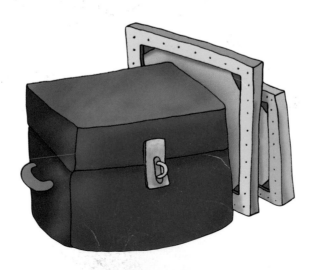

Caillou saw a big trunk
full of old hats at the back of the attic.
It looked like a treasure chest.
"I want to play in the attic, Daddy.
Do you want to stay with me?"

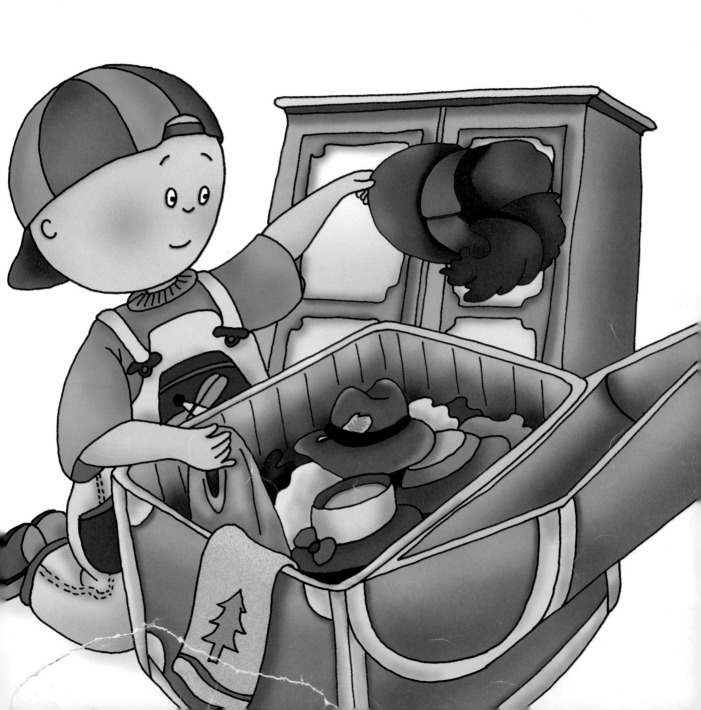

We gratefully acknowledge the financial support of BPIDP, SODEC and the Canada Council for the Arts.

Text: Joceline Sanschagrin
Illustrations: Claude Lapierre

© 2000 Chouette Publishing

Canadian Cataloguing in Publication Data
Sanschagrin, Joceline, 1950-
Caillou, the wolf
(North star)
Translation of: Caillou, le loup.
For children aged 3 and up.

ISBN 2-89450-178-1

1. Fear – Juvenile literature. I. Lapierre, Claude, 1942-   . II. Title. III. Title: Wolf.
IV. Series.

BF723.F4S2613 2000   j155.4'1246   C00-940875-4

Printed in Canada
1 0 9 8 7 6 5 4 3 2

Table of Contents

Chapter 1
Financial Aid Basics

Applying for financial aid can be intimidating and confusing. That's why it is very important that you and your parent(s) learn as much as you can about the basics of financial aid and how the financial aid process works. The more you know, the better. Once you and your parent(s) familiarize yourselves with the basics of financial aid, the process is relatively simple. The first step towards understanding financial aid is to read this chapter and then meet with a financial aid administrator at a local college or institution you plan to attend.

Chapter 1: Financial Aid Basics covers:
- What is Financial Aid?
- Types of Financial Aid
- How financial aid is awarded
  - Financial Need
  - Calculating Financial Need
  - Merit-Based Aid
- Free Application for Federal Student Aid (FAFSA)
- Financial Aid PROFILE Form
- Financial Aid Package (Award Letter)
- External "Outside" Awards
- Financial Aid Disbursement
- Renewing Financial Aid

What is Financial Aid?

Financial aid makes higher education possible for almost every student. Its purpose is to help you and your parent(s) pay for your school expenses (i.e. tuition, room & board, books and supplies, laboratory fees, etc.). Financial aid is available from many sources such as the federal government, state education agencies, colleges/universities, businesses, private organizations, and individuals.

Types of Financial Aid

Financial aid is awarded in the form of:

- Scholarships
  Scholarships are considered gift aid (FREE money) and do not have to be repaid. Some scholarships are awarded on a one-time basis, while others are renewable. Renewable scholarships may be guaranteed for a student's entire undergraduate or graduate study. However, the scholarship recipient must abide by the scholarship provider's rules and guidelines to remain eligible for the scholarship.

  Scholarships are often categorized as:

  o National Awards
    National awards are very competitive and usually have several restrictions such as majoring in a specific career field and/or test scores. National awards may have other restrictions, but are not restricted to a student's geographic location (i.e. region, state, city) or type of institution. Typically, national awards offer larger monetary scholarships, in which eligible candidates, nationwide, compete for this type of award. For these reasons, national awards are considered to be very competitive.

  o Regional Awards
    Regional awards are very competitive and are restricted to a student's geographic location, which consist of several states. Other restrictions may include majoring in a specific career field, ethnic background, test score(s), gender, etc.

  o State Awards
    State awards are competitive and are restricted to students that are residents of a specific state. Other restrictions may include enrollment at a state school, majoring in a specific career field, ethnic background, test score(s), gender, etc.

  o Local Awards
    Local awards are 'less' competitive than national, regional, and state awards, because of their restrictions and the limited number of eligible applicants. Local awards are usually restricted to students that are residents of a specific city, county, or district. Other restrictions may also include enrollment at a specific high school, majoring in a specific field of study, ethnic background, test score(s), gender, etc. Typically, local awards are less than $1,000, not well publicized, overlooked, and awarded on a one-time basis.

For example:

1. A scholarship for African-American students, residents of Chicago, Illinois, majoring in Aviation, with a 3.5 grade point average, will probably have very few applicants, which makes this sample award "less" competitive.

o   Institutional Awards
    Institutional awards are competitive and are restricted to students that attend a specific school. Institutions require that students must be accepted for admission before they are eligible to apply for their institutional award(s). Usually, Institutional Aid is awarded to students who have demonstrated financial need. However, some Institutional Aid is awarded to students based on their merit and/or academic achievements. These awards may have other restrictions such as majoring in a specific field of study, ethnic background, test score(s), gender, etc.

o   International Awards
    International awards are competitive and are restricted to a student's nationality, citizenship, or country of residency. These awards may have other restrictions such as enrollment at a specific institution, field of study, etc.

•   Grants
    Grants are considered gift aid and do not have to be repaid. Grants are usually awarded on a first-come, first-serve basis to students usually based on financial need and on a one-time basis. However, some grants are renewable as long as there are available funds and the student remains eligible by following the grant provider's rules and guidelines. Three common grant providers are: federal government, state education agencies, and institutions.

•   Fellowships
    Fellowships are considered gift aid and do not have to be repaid. Fellowships are highly competitive with a typical one or two year commitment. Fellowships are usually awarded to graduate students for post-graduate study, research, special employment experiences, special projects, enrollment at a specific school, and more. Typically, a fellowship will pay for the student's tuition, fees, room & board, books and supplies, etc. Most fellowships will also provide students with a monthly stipend for living expenses.

•   Assistantships
    Assistantships are considered self-help aid. They offer graduate students the opportunity to perform teaching and/or research duties, in which they are given a full or partial tuition waiver and a monthly stipend. Usually, there is a limit to the number of hours a student can work per week.

•   Work-Study Program
    Work-study programs are considered self-help aid that is awarded on a first-come, first-serve basis to students usually based on financial need. The purpose of this program is to provide part-time employment to undergraduate and graduate students to help them earn money to pay for personal and educational expenses, during their enrollment in school. The money earned does not have to be repaid.

- Educational Loans
  Educational loans are considered self-help aid. A loan is borrowed money that must be repaid with interest. These loans are offered through a variety of sources such as: federal and state governments, institutions, employers, private lenders, banks, credit unions, and family members. There are four kinds of educational loans: Student Loans, Parent Loans for Undergraduate Students (PLUS), Consolidation Loans, and Private Loans (Alternative Loans).

Note: Most students will use a combination of scholarships, grants, work-study, loans, and family contributions to pay for their postsecondary education (i.e. college). Students that have been convicted of drug distribution or possession, or other felonies may be ineligible for certain financial aid (i.e. Federal Aid).

How financial aid is awarded
Financial aid is awarded to students based on:
- Financial Need
- Merit / Academic Achievements

Financial Need
Financial aid is usually awarded to students on the basis of financial need. Financial need is the difference between: Cost of Attendance (COA) and Expected Family Contribution (EFC).

- Cost of Attendance (COA)
  The financial aid office of each school will calculate an **estimate** of how much it will cost you, the student, to attend their school for one academic year. Your COA will primarily depend on your residency (in-state or out-of-state student status) and major (field of study). However, your estimated COA should assist you and your parent(s) in planning a budget. Your COA will vary from one school to another.

  Estimated COA will typically include:
  - Tuition and Fees
  - Room and Board
  - Books and Supplies
  - Travel/Transportation
  - Personal Expenses
  - Miscellaneous Expenses

  In many cases there is a standard fixed budget amount for some of these categories. For example, the budget amount for travel may vary depending on the student's home state. Room and board expenses may be reduced and travel expenses increased for commuter students living at home or off-campus. If you are interested in calculating an estimated COA for attending a particular school, you should contact the school's admission and financial aid offices to request a school catalog, housing brochure, and information regarding other expenses (i.e. books, student activity fees, etc.). For information on additional fees for certain academic programs, you should contact the academic department. Remember, this is only an estimate; actual costs may differ from the school's estimated COA once school starts.

- Expected Family Contribution (EFC)
The Expected Family Contribution (EFC) is the amount of funding you and your parent(s) are expected to contribute towards your college education. The EFC is an **estimate** of the amount of money you and your parent(s) could reasonably contribute toward college costs. However, this amount may not equal the amount your family can actually contribute. The EFC is the sum of the student and parent contribution:

EFC = Student Contribution + Parent Contribution

Your EFC is calculated by completing the Free Application for Federal Student Aid (FAFSA). The FAFSA is used by the U.S. Department of Education to determine your Expected Family Contribution (EFC) and eligibility for certain Federal Aid Programs.   In order to receive financial aid from the federal government, you must complete the FAFSA. Many state education agencies and institutions also use the information submitted on your FAFSA to determine your eligibility for State and Institutional Aid.

In calculating your EFC for one academic year, the following factors are considered:
- Income (Taxable and Non-taxable)
- Assets (i.e. stocks, bonds, savings, and business assets)
- Number of Children in Household
- Certain Debts
- Unusual Circumstances

The federal formula approved by Congress to calculate the EFC is called the Federal Methodology (FM). The Federal Methodology is used to determine your eligibility for Federal Aid. Some schools rely on a different formula for awarding their Institutional Aid, which is called the Institutional Methodology (IM). Some schools use various Institutional Methodology formulas.

Calculating Financial Need

Your COA and EFC is used in the following equation to determine your financial need:

	Cost of Attendance (COA)
-	Expected Family Contribution (EFC)
=	Financial Need

After the financial aid administrator inputs the appropriate numbers into this equation, your total will determine whether or not you have demonstrated financial need.

Example:

John Doe will attend AvScholars Technical School in the Fall of 2006. The Cost of Attendance (COA) at AvScholars Technical School is $10,000, and John Doe's Expected Family Contribution (EFC) is $2,300.

	$10,000	COA
	- $2,300	EFC
	= $7,700	Financial Need

In this example, John Doe needs $7,700 to help pay for his college costs. Therefore, John Doe has demonstrated financial need.

If you have demonstrated financial need, the financial aid office of each school will try to meet this demonstrated financial need through a "financial aid package." Your financial aid package may include various types of financial aid such as scholarships, grants, work-study, and/or loans. Financial aid administrators may also refer to parts of your financial aid as Need-Based and Non-Need Based Aid. Financial aid awarded to students based on financial need is called Need-Based Aid. The purpose of Need-Based aid is to supplement the family's contribution, not to replace it. Non-Need Based Aid (a.k.a. Merit-Based Aid) is awarded to students based on their merit or academic achievements such as test scores, talents, etc.

Note: If the financial aid administrator calculated and determined that you did not demonstrate financial need, you may be eligible for Non-Need Based student loans and possible Merit-Based Aid.

Merit-Based Aid
Financial aid awarded to students based on their merit or academic achievements is called Merit-Based Aid (Non-Need Based Aid). Merit-Based Aid does not require students to demonstrate financial need. This type of aid is awarded in the form of scholarships, grants, and fellowships. You should inquire about Merit-Based Aid awarded to students at the school(s) you are interested in attending. Remember, your state's education agencies may also award Merit-Based Aid to students.

Merit-Based Aid is usually awarded to students based:
- Test Scores (i.e. ACT, SAT, GMAT, etc.)
- Gender
- Field of Study (i.e. Teacher, Flight Training, Medicine, etc.)
- Enrollment at a Specific School
- Geographic Area (i.e. City, Region, District, County, etc.)
- Leadership Abilities
- Disability Impairments (i.e. Blindness, Hearing Impairment, etc.)
- Athletic Talents
- Ethnic or Racial Background
- Religious Affiliation
- Artistic Talents (i.e. Musician, Dancing, etc.)
- Graduate/Professional Studies

Free Application for Federal Student Aid (FAFSA)

The first step in applying for financial aid is to complete the Free Application for Federal Student Aid (FAFSA), which is one of the most important applications of any financial aid process. The FAFSA is used by the U.S. Department of Education (www.ed.gov) to determine your Expected Family Contribution (EFC) and eligibility for Federal Aid through the Student Financial Aid Program (SFA) administered by the federal government. Many state education agencies and institutions also use the information submitted on your FAFSA to determine your eligibility for State and Institutional Aid. Some state education agencies and institutions may require you to fill out additional forms to determine your eligibility for their State and Institutional Aid. You must complete the FAFSA, each year, to be eligible for Federal Aid.

The Student Financial Aid Program (SFA) consists of:
- Federal Pell Grants
- Campus-Based Programs
  - Federal Supplemental Opportunity Grants (FSEOG)
  - Federal Work-Study (FWS)
  - Federal Perkins Loans
- Federal Family Education Loan (FFEL) Program
  - Federal Stafford Loans (Subsidized and Unsubsidized)
  - Federal PLUS (Parent Loan for Undergraduate Students) Loans
- William D. Ford Federal Direct Loan (Direct Loan) Program
  - Direct Loans (Subsidized and Unsubsidized)
  - Direct PLUS Loans

The Student Guide is the most comprehensive resource on student financial aid from the U.S. Department of Education. This guide will provide you with detailed information on: student eligibility, financial need, dependency status, how to apply, special circumstances, withdrawals, deadlines, types of Student Federal Aid (award amounts, interest, etc.), borrower responsibilities and rights, important terms, telephone numbers, useful web sites, and more. You can download a copy of *The Student Guide* from the U.S. Department of Education's web site at www.studentaid.ed.gov/guide, which is available in English and Spanish. You will need the Adobe Acrobat Reader (www.adobe.com) to view and print this document.

When to Apply

It is important to submit your completed FAFSA as soon as possible **after** January 1st of each year. Do not sign (in print or electronic format), date, or send your application before January 1st. If you apply before January 1st, your application will not be processed.

Do not wait until you have been admitted to a school (i.e. college) to complete the FAFSA. Many state education agencies and institutions also use the information submitted on your FAFSA to determine your eligibility for State and Institutional Aid. State education agencies and institutions typically award their financial aid (i.e. scholarships, grants, work-study) on a first-come, first-serve basis until all funds are exhausted. If you delay submitting your FAFSA, it will affect your chances of receiving the maximum amount of financial aid you may have been eligible to receive for the upcoming academic year. Therefore, you should submit your FAFSA early, **after** January 1st, to meet State and Institutional Aid deadline dates. It is a good idea to contact your state education agencies and each school's financial aid office for specific financial aid deadline dates. State education agencies deadline dates are also listed on the FAFSA.

Note: You must reapply for Federal Aid each year. Also, if you decide to change schools, your financial aid does not automatically transfer to the new school. Check with your new school to find out what steps you must take to continue receiving financial aid.

Completing the FAFSA

Completing the FAFSA is an easy process. The forms are very similar to income tax forms and require much of the same information.   It is important to read the instructions carefully when completing the FAFSA or the Renewal FAFSA.

The following materials are needed to complete the FAFSA:
- Student's State ID or Driver's License
- Social Security Card
- W-2 Forms and other records of money earned (usually from the previous year)
- Previous years U.S. income tax return (IRS Form 1040, 1040A, or 1040EZ)
- Records of untaxed income, such as Social Security benefits, AFDC or ADC, child support, welfare, pensions, military subsistence allowances, and veterans benefits
- Current bank statements
- Current mortgage information (if applicable)
- Business and/or farm records (if applicable)
- Records of stocks, bonds, mutual funds, CDs, and other investments (if applicable)
- Medical and/or dental expenses during the past year not covered by medical insurance

You should pay special attention to any questions regarding income, since most errors occur in this area. It is important to save all the information and materials used to complete your FAFSA, because you may need them later to verify the information reported on your FAFSA. The process of proving that your information is correct is called verification. If you cannot or do not provide the document(s) requested for verification, you will not receive financial aid from the Student Financial Aid Program (SFA), and you may not receive financial aid from other sources (i.e. state education agencies, institutions, etc.). You should make a photocopy of your completed FAFSA (or print out a copy of your FAFSA Express or FAFSA on the Web application) before you submit it, for your own records.

Tips
When starting the application process, you and your parents should:
- Read all the instructions.
- Make a practice worksheet.
- Use a pencil on your practice worksheet so you can easily change your answers.
- Copy the answers neatly and carefully on to the original form.
- Answer every question. Follow the instructions on what to do if a question does not apply to you.
- Print neat and legible.
- Give accurate information.
- Double-check your answers to make sure they are complete and accurate. Be sure you have provided the necessary signatures electronically or on paper.

Need Help

If you have any questions or problems with completing the FAFSA, help is available. Making errors can cause delays in processing your FAFSA.

You should consider the following **FREE** resources for help:

- High school guidance counselors.

- Financial Aid Administrators.
  Most financial aid administrators at a nearby college or university can assist you and your parent(s) with completing the FAFSA, which is dependent on their availability and workload.

- Federal Student Aid Information Center (FSAIC).
  For information on any federal student financial aid programs or assistance in completing the FAFSA, you can call the Federal Student Aid Information Center at 800-4-FED-AID (800-433-3243) or 800-730-8913 (TTY) for the hearing impaired.

- U.S. Department of Education Web Sites.
  There are several web sites by the U.S. Department of Education that can assist you and your parent(s) with completing the FAFSA:
  - Help completing the FAFSA (www.ed.gov/prog_info/SFA/FAFSA/)
  - Student aid home page (www.ed.gov/studentaid)
  - Government Services (Including Education) available to students (www.students.gov)

How to Submit the FAFSA

There are four ways to submit your completed FAFSA:

- *FAFSA on the Web* (www.fafsa.ed.gov)
  FAFSA on the Web is a free U.S. Department of Education web site, where you can complete and submit your FAFSA online.

- *FAFSA Express*
  FAFSA Express is a free software program that allows you to apply for federal student aid from your home computer or from a computer at a central location such as a high school, postsecondary school, public library, or local Educational Opportunity Center that uses *FAFSA Express*. *FAFSA Express* can be used only on a personal computer equipped with a modem. If you wish to apply using *FAFSA Express*, you can order diskettes at 800-801-0576 or download a copy of the software program from the U.S. Department of Education's web site at www.ed.gov/offices/OSFAP/Students/apply/fexpress.html.

- Electronically
  Your school may be able to submit your FAFSA electronically. Contact the school's financial aid office to inquire about submitting your FAFSA electronically.

- Paper FAFSA
  The paper FAFSA should be available after mid-November of each year. You can obtain a paper version of the FAFSA from your high school, the financial aid office at any college or university,

public library, or the Federal Student Aid Information Center by calling 1-800-4-FED-AID (1-800-433-3243). If you apply by mail, you should send your completed application in the envelope provided within the FAFSA application packet. This envelope will ensure that your application reaches the correct address.

What happens after submitting your completed FAFSA

Once your FAFSA has been received and processed by the federal processor, you will receive a Student Aid Report (SAR) within 48 hours after filing the FAFSA on the web or 4-6 weeks after filing a paper FAFSA. The SAR summarizes the information you provided on the FAFSA, in which the federal processor reviewed, analyzed, and calculated your Expected Family Contribution (EFC). This figure will serve as a guideline to determine your eligibility for Federal, State, and Institutional Aid.

When you receive your SAR, you must review it carefully for accuracy and correct any discrepancies. If you need to change or make corrections to your SAR, you should promptly submit your corrections online or by mail. If your FAFSA was completed without any problems, your EFC will be printed above your Data Release Number (DRN) in the upper right hand corner.

Your SAR will be mailed to the schools' financial aid offices that you listed on the FAFSA. Each school's financial aid office will use the information provided on the SAR to estimate your financial need and determine your eligibility for Federal and Institutional aid.

If it has been more than four weeks since you submitted your FAFSA and you have not received a response, you can check on the status of your application through the *FAFSA on the Web* at www.fafsa.ed.gov (even if you did not apply using *FAFSA on the Web*), or by contacting the Federal Student Aid Information Center at 800-4-FED-AID (800-433-3243) or 800-730-8913 (TTY) for the hearing impaired.

Financial Aid PROFILE Form (if necessary)

Some schools and scholarship providers require that you complete the Financial Aid PROFILE form in addition to the FAFSA. The PROFILE form is a financial aid application service provided by the College Board. The PROFILE form asks more specific questions (not generally covered by the FAFSA form) to determine your eligibility for *nonfederal student aid* such as Institutional Aid.

There is a nonrefundable registration fee plus an additional charge for each school or organization that you want to receive your Profile form information. You should be able to obtain copies of the PROFILE form from your high school guidance office, financial aid office, or the College Board's web site at www.collegeboard.com. The Financial Aid Profile form can also be completed online. You can learn more about the Profile form, including which schools require financial aid applicants to complete the Profile at The College Board's web site. You also have the option of contacting each school's financial aid office that you applied to for admission, and ask if you are required to complete the PROFILE form in addition to the FAFSA.

Financial Aid Package (a.k.a. Award Letter)

Once you have been admitted to a school, their financial aid office will create a financial aid package (award letter) for you to help meet your financial need for the upcoming academic school year. Financial aid packages are sent soon after admission letters are mailed to first-year and transfer students. The financial aid package is sometimes called an "aid package" because it may include both self-help (i.e. loans and employment) and gift aid (i.e. scholarships and grants). The total financial aid package a student receives cannot exceed the school's estimated cost of attendance.

Your financial aid package will indicate your estimated Cost of Attendance (COA), Expected Family Contribution (EFC), terms and conditions, and the types of financial aid and award amounts. Students with greater financial needs are typically offered a combination of self-help and gift aid. Students with less financial needs are typically offered self-help aid. Many colleges and universities offer scholarships and grants to freshmen and sophomore students, and then add on more student loans in their junior and senior years.

Each school's financial aid package will offer different types of financial aid and award amounts. You will receive different levels of financial aid based on your individual circumstances such as: your EFC, demonstrated financial need, state residency (i.e. in-state or out-of-state student), enrollment status (full or part-time), whether or not you will attend school for a full academic year or less, the school's financial aid policies, and availability of financial aid funds. Your financial aid package may be based on the assumption that you will enroll as a full-time student for each term (i.e. semesters). If you enroll as a part-time student, some of your financial aid may be reduced or cancelled. All of these variables will affect your financial aid package.

Financial aid packages typically include aid from a combination of sources and programs such as:
* Scholarships and Grants (Gift Aid)
  Sources: Federal and State Government, Institutions, Private Foundations, Organizations, Employers, etc.
* Loans (Self-Help Aid)
  Sources: Federal and State Government, Institutions, Employers, Private Lenders, etc.
* Work-Study (Self-Help Aid)
  Sources: Federal and State Government, and Institutions

The financial aid package is generally broken down by term (i.e. semester). When you receive your financial aid package, you and your parent(s) must read the instructions carefully to make sure that you understand all the terms and conditions to decide if you want to accept all, parts, or none of the financial aid offered. You do not have to accept all parts of the financial aid listed on your award letter. However, if you decline some parts of the financial aid awarded to you (i.e. work-study or loan), the school will not replace it with a scholarship or grant. Generally, the financial aid office has already awarded you the maximum amount of financial aid. If you have any questions about your financial aid package, you should contact the school's financial aid office. It is important to make sure that all of your questions are answered, before declining any parts of your financial aid package.

Additional forms (i.e. loan applications) may be included with your financial aid package. If additional forms are included, it is important to complete all of the forms (as necessary). If the school's financial aid office (FAO) requests additional documentation, you should send them as soon as possible. If the financial aid office does not receive the requested documents, your application may be considered incomplete. Failure to submit or complete the required forms will cause a delay in the processing of your financial aid, and possibly result in you receiving reduced financial aid.

Your parents will have to complete additional loan application to receive a Direct PLUS or FFEL PLUS (Parent Loan for Undergraduate Students) Loan. Loan applications may be included with your financial aid package or you may have to contact a lending institution to request a loan application. Your school's financial aid office may have a listing of lenders.

The Deadline

After reviewing your financial aid package, you must sign, date, and return a copy to the school's financial aid office by a certain deadline date specified in the letter. It is important that you carefully read all the instructions and include all requested documentation and complete additional forms (if required). Failure to respond by the deadline date may result in your financial aid being denied or reduced. A portion of your reduced financial aid may be offered to another student that has financial need. You should make a copy of everything for your records, before you mail them back to your school's financial aid office.

If you have been admitted to more than one school, you will receive a financial aid package from each school. You should review and compare the financial aid packages among the various schools. Once you have decided upon the school you will attend, you should notify the other schools that admitted you to inform them that you are not going to attend their school. This gesture will allow the other school(s) to offer admission and financial aid to another eligible student interested in continuing his/her education.

Unmet Need

The financial aid office tries to create a financial aid package that comes as close as possible to meeting your financial need. Unfortunately, financial aid funds are limited. The school's financial aid office may not be able to provide you with financial aid to meet your entire demonstrated financial need.

In some cases, the school may tell you that you have an "Unmet Need." Unmet Need indicates that you must obtain financial aid from other sources, if you want to attend their school.

Funds for Unmet Need can be obtained from:
1. Summer employment earnings.
2. Federal Parent Loan for Undergraduate Students (PLUS).
3. Alternative loans (Private loans).
4. Institutional loans.
5. Other options (i.e. Home equity loan, Employer loan, Prepaid Tuition Plan, etc.).

Special/Unusual Circumstances

If your family's situation has changed since you filed the FAFSA, you should contact the school's financial aid office to inform them about your special/unusual circumstance(s) and to update your records. In some cases, a financial aid administrator may adjust your financial aid package, if he/she finds that special/unusual circumstances exist based on the documentation you provided. However, the financial aid administrator does not have to make an adjustment, if he/she believes no change is necessary. Please note that the financial aid administrator's decision is final and cannot be appealed to the U.S. Department of Education.

Some special/unusual circumstances may include:
- Medical expenses (because of a serious or long term illness)
- A disabled member of the family
- Unemployment
- Separation or divorce
- A parent who is disabled, retired, or deceased
- More than one child in college at the same time, or a parent who is a full time student
- Debt (Not consumer debt)

External ("Outside") Awards

Federal regulations and school policies require the financial aid office (FAO) to consider all sources of financial aid received by students when determining their eligibility for financial aid. You are required to report any external ("outside") award, regardless of amount, in writing to the school's financial aid office. An external award that you receive will be taken into consideration when calculating your financial aid package, which is often counted 100% towards meeting your financial need. If you receive an external award not listed in your financial aid package, the financial aid office is required to re-evaluate your financial aid package and possibly reduce certain financial aid to remain in compliance with federal regulations and school policies.

If the external award affects your existing financial aid package, the financial aid office may have to make adjustments by reducing some of your financial aid, and you may owe money. Reductions in your financial aid package are typically made in the following order: any unmet need, self-help aid, and then need-based aid (i.e. grants). The FAO will allow external awards to replace unmet need or self-help aid to a maximum of the loan or work-study in your financial aid package. Every effort should be made not to reduce Need-Based Aid unless required by federal or state regulations and school policies. An external award cannot be used to replace a part of your Expected Family's Contribution.

External awards include, not limited to:
- Prepaid Tuition Plans
- Employer benefits
- VA Educational Benefits
- Any Tuition Benefits
- Non-Service Fellowships
- Vocational Rehabilitation Benefits
- RA Benefits
- Graduate Assistantships
- Social Security Educational Benefits
- ROTC Benefits
- Private Scholarships and Grants (from private and civic organizations, businesses, etc.)

It is up to you to decide whether or not to inform your school's financial aid office about any external award(s), not listed in your financial aid package. If you do not notify your school's FAO, they may eventually find out about your external award. Usually, this occurs whenever the organization submits the scholarship check directly to your school. If this is the case, they will make adjustments as necessary. Avoid unpleasant surprises of receiving reduced aid or owing money back to either the government or your school. If you are unsure about how your external award(s) will affect your financial aid package, you should contact your school's financial aid office to discuss your situation.

Financial Aid Disbursement

The financial aid office administers and oversees how financial aid is allocated to their school's students. They do not disburse any checks. The school's Bursar's Office (Business Office) is responsible for processing and disbursing all financial aid. The financial aid disbursement usually begins one week prior to the start of classes and is scheduled regularly thereafter according to the school's disbursement schedule. Before your financial aid is disbursed, you must fulfill certain enrollment criteria. It is very important that you read your school's *Financial Aid Guide* to learn about the enrollment criteria to receive financial aid and the financial aid disbursement process.

Renewing Financial Aid

You must reapply for financial aid each year by submitting a FAFSA or Renewal FAFSA to continue receiving Federal, State, and/or Institutional aid. The Renewal FAFSA has fewer questions to answer. Most of the information on the form will be pre-filled with the information you provided the previous year. You will only have to add new information and update any information that has changed since the previous year. As your financial situation changes each year (i.e. income, assets, marital status, medical expenses, etc.), your financial aid package will be adjusted each year.

Eligibility for financial aid based on financial need will be based on your current financial status each year. You must continue to demonstrate financial need and satisfactory academic progress to remain eligible for financial aid based on need. It is very important that you read your school's *Financial Aid Guide* to learn about the school's policies such as Financial Aid Probation and Suspension, Reinstatement, Appeal Process, Fee Deferments, Disbursements, Refund and Repayments on Financial Aid, etc.

Renewal FAFSA must be received **before** March 1st at the central processing office to be considered for priority funding. If you filed the FAFSA online in prior years, you should have received a Personal Identification Number (PIN) in the mail with renewal instructions. If you do not have a PIN, visit the FAFSA's web site at www.fafsa.ed.gov and follow the instructions for receiving a PIN. You may use your PIN to apply for financial aid online at www.fafsa.ed.gov **after** January 1st for the following academic year. In order to sign the FAFSA form electronically, both you and your parent(s) must have a PIN. If you have any questions about the Renewal FAFSA, contact your school's financial aid office or the Federal Student Aid Information Center at 800-4-FED-AID (800-433-3243) or 800-730-8913 (TTY) for the hearing impaired.

What's Next?

Now that you have a better understanding about the basics of financial aid, you should start documenting your qualifications to help you search and apply for scholarships. Your next step is Chapter 2: The Workbook.

Chapter 2
The Workbook

Chapter 2: The Workbook is divided into several parts. Each part focuses on different components of the scholarship search and application process. It is important that you identify and document as much information about yourself and your family. The more information you document about you and your family, the more scholarships you are likely to identify and apply for in which you may have overlooked.

Chapter 2: The Workbook consists of eight parts:
- Part I: Personal Profile
- Part II: Family Background
- Part III: Educational Background
- Part IV: Work Experiences
- Part V: Extracurricular Activities
- Part VI: References
- Part VII: Resume Template
- Part VIII: Track Forms

Part I
Personal Profile

Part I: Personal Profile will help you identify and document information about your educational and career goals. Many scholarships have certain restrictions and eligibility requirements that may apply to your geographic location, gender, test score(s), financial need, field of study, etc.

Part I: Personal Profile will help you identify and document:
- Personal Information
- Educational Status
- Financial Aid Status
- Educational and Career Goals
- Strengths and Weaknesses
- College Plans

Personal Information

List general information about yourself.

Name: _____

Present Address

Address:_____

City: _____   State/Province: _____   Zip/Postal Code: _____

Telephone: _____   Email: _____

Permanent Address

Address:_____

City: _____   State/Province: _____   Zip/Postal Code: _____

Telephone: _____   Email: _____

Social Security Number: _____   Gender: ❑ Male   ❑ Female

Date of Birth: _____   Age: _____

Place of Birth (City & State or Country): _____

Martial Status: ❑ Single   ❑ Married   ❑ Divorced   ❑ Widowed   ❑ Separated

Citizenship: ❑ US Citizen   ❑ US Permanent, Legal Resident   ❑ Foreign National

Educational Status

Select your current educational status.

High School:
❑ Freshman
❑ Sophomore
❑ Junior
❑ Senior

College:
❑ Freshman (1st Year)
❑ Sophomore
❑ Junior
❑ Senior

Graduate:
❑ Master
❑ Doctorate
❑ Professional Development

Other:
❑ Returning Adult
❑ Other: _____

Financial Aid Status

What level of study will you need financial aid? For example, if you need a scholarship for your Sophomore year of college, choose "Sophomore." If you're not pursuing a degree, select "Non-degree." Choose "Returning Adult " if you're returning to school after a lengthy interruption for work, family, or other reasons.

College:
❑ Freshman
❑ Sophomore
❑ Junior
❑ Senior

Graduate:
❑ Master
❑ Doctorate
❑ Professional Development

Other:
❑ Returning Adult
❑ Non-degree
❑ Other: _____

Educational and Career Goals

What are your educational and career goals? Think of how you would like to pursue your career goals. You should also consider the steps it will take to help you achieve your goals.

_____

_____

_____

_____

_____

_____

_____

_____

_____

_____

_____

_____

_____

_____

_____

_____

_____

_____

_____

_____

_____

_____

_____

_____

_____

_____

_____

_____

Strengths and Weaknesses

List your strengths and weaknesses or any obstacles that may prevent you from doing your best. Try to turn a negative into a positive. Review your weaknesses and ask yourself, "How can I overcome my weaknesses to help me achieve my goals."

<table>
<tr><td>Strengths</td><td>Weaknesses</td></tr>
<tr><td>1. _____</td><td>1. _____</td></tr>
<tr><td>2. _____</td><td>2. _____</td></tr>
<tr><td>3. _____</td><td>3. _____</td></tr>
<tr><td>4. _____</td><td>4. _____</td></tr>
<tr><td>5. _____</td><td>5. _____</td></tr>
<tr><td>6. _____</td><td>6. _____</td></tr>
<tr><td>7. _____</td><td>7. _____</td></tr>
<tr><td>8. _____</td><td>8. _____</td></tr>
<tr><td>9. _____</td><td>9. _____</td></tr>
<tr><td>10. _____</td><td>10. _____</td></tr>
<tr><td>11. _____</td><td>11. _____</td></tr>
<tr><td>12. _____</td><td>12. _____</td></tr>
</table>

Additional Notes

_____

_____

_____

_____

_____

_____

_____

_____

_____

_____

_____

_____

College Plans

Field of Study

List the field of study that you plan to pursue as a career. Many scholarships are available to students based on their field of study or particular career interest.

1. _____   7. _____
2. _____   8. _____
3. _____   9. _____
4. _____   10. _____
5. _____   11. _____
6. _____   12. _____

Educational Information

List the schools you plan to apply to for admission.

1. _____   7. _____
2. _____   8. _____
3. _____   9. _____
4. _____   10. _____
5. _____   11. _____
6. _____   12. _____

Type of School

Select the type of school(s) you plan to attend: (Select all that apply.)

❏ Public School   ❏ Trade, Technical, or Vocational School   ❏ Historical Black College/University
❏ Private School   ❏ Two-year Community / Junior College   ❏ Hispanic Serving Institution
                         ❏ Four-year College / University   ❏ Tribal School Serving the Community
                         ❏ Graduate School
                         ❏ Other: _____

Enrollment Status
You plan to attend school: ❏ Full-time   ❏ Part-time

School Location: ❏ In-State   ❏ Out-of-State: (Where) _____

                              ❏ Aboard: (Country) _____

Part II
Family Background

Part II: Family Background will help you identify and document information about you and your family. You may need your parent(s) and/or grandparent(s) assistance to help answer some questions. Many scholarships have certain restrictions and eligibility requirements that may apply to you as well as your parents and/or grandparent(s).

If your parents are divorced, you should be aware of both parents' background and affiliations. If one or both of your parents are deceased, you may be eligible for some awards based on their background, past memberships, and/or affiliations.

Part II: Family Background will help you identify and document:
- Parents Information
- Family Financial Data
- Organizations or Club Affiliation
- Banking Institutions
- Employers
- Military Affiliation
- Ethnic/Racial Background
- Disability Impairment
- Religious Affiliation

Parents Information

List general information about your parents.

Father

Name: _____

Occupation: _____

Employer: _____

Address: _____

City: _____   State/Province: _____   Zip/Postal Code: _____

Telephone: _____   Email: _____

Mother

Name: _____

Occupation: _____

Employer: _____

Address: _____

City: _____   State/Province: _____   Zip/Postal Code: _____

Telephone: _____   Email: _____

Family Financial Data

List your family's financial information. Some scholarships are awarded to students based on their families' income and circumstances. Some scholarship providers may request a copy of you and/or your parent(s) most recent Federal Income Tax return - Form 1040. This information is used to verify your family's income and financial need. Remember, some scholarships are awarded to students based on financial need.

Number of People in Parents' Household
Enter the number of people in your parents' household. Include: yourself (even if you
do not live with your parents), your parents, and your brothers and/or sisters.   _____

Number of Family Members in College
Enter total number of family members attending a college, vocational, or trade school at least
part-time in a program that leads to a college degree or certificate, including yourself.   _____

What is your family's total gross income?
Enter your parents' total wages, your wages, salaries, or other earnings, including net business $_____.00
profits, Social Security benefits or Disability Insurance, Child Support Received, Veterans or
Military Benefits, etc.

Organizations or Club Affiliation

List the name of all organizations, unions, and clubs you, your parent(s), or grandparent(s) are members. Example: Beta Club, Math Club, ALPA, AFL-CIO, Fraternal Order of Police, Links, etc. Some scholarships are offered to members and/or their children.

1. _____   7. _____
2. _____   8. _____
3. _____   9. _____
4. _____   10. _____
5. _____   11. _____
6. _____   12. _____

Banking Institutions

List the name of all banking institution(s) or credit union(s) in which you, your parent(s), or grandparent(s) have a bank account. Some scholarships are offered to eligible account holders and/or their children.

1. _____   7. _____
2. _____   8. _____
3. _____   9. _____
4. _____   10. _____
5. _____   11. _____
6. _____   12. _____

Employers

List the name of all employers in which you and your parent(s) are employed. Some scholarships are offered to eligible employees and/or their children. You may also be eligible for a scholarship, if one of your parents died or was disabled while working such as a firefighter, police officer, or other public servant.

1. _____   7. _____
2. _____   8. _____
3. _____   9. _____
4. _____   10. _____
5. _____   11. _____
6. _____   12. _____

Military Affiliation

List all of your family's military affiliation. If you and your parent(s) served in a branch of the U.S. Armed Forces, you may be eligible for certain educational benefits and/or scholarships through the Veteran Affairs Educational Benefits Programs.

❑ Air Force   ❑ National Guard
❑ Army   ❑ Coast Guard
❑ Marines   ❑ Reserves
❑ Navy   ❑ ROTC: Indicate the service: _____

Other:_____
_____
_____

Ethnic/Racial Background

List all of your family's ethnic or racial background. Some scholarships are available to students of a particular ethnic or racial background. If your family's background includes several ethnic or racial groups, be sure to list all that apply. (i.e. African American, Hispanic, Greek, Italian, Japanese, Native-American, Puerto Rican, Polish, etc.).

1. _____   7. _____
2. _____   8. _____
3. _____   9. _____
4. _____   10. _____
5. _____   11. _____
6. _____   12. _____

Disability Impairment

Select and list any disability impairments and/or medical conditions that apply to you and/or your parent(s). Some scholarships are available to students or their parents that have disability impairments or medical conditions. (i.e. asthma, dyslexia, neurological speech disorder, etc.).

❑ Blind / Visual Impairment: _____   ❑ Learning Impairment:_____
❑ Deaf / Hearing Impairment: _____   ❑ Mental Impairment: _____
❑ Developmental Impairment:_____   ❑ Physical Impairment: _____
❑ Disabled Parent: _____   ❑ Respiratory Impairment:_____

Other:_____
_____
_____

Religious Affiliation

List your family's religious affiliation (i.e. Baptist, Buddhist, Catholic, Christian, Jewish, Muslim, Protestant, etc.). Some scholarships are available to students of a particular religious faith.

1. _____
2. _____
3. _____
4. _____
5. _____
6. _____

7. _____
8. _____
9. _____
10. _____
11. _____
12. _____

Additional Notes

_____
_____
_____
_____
_____
_____
_____
_____
_____
_____
_____
_____
_____
_____
_____
_____
_____
_____
_____
_____
_____

Part III
Educational Background

Part III: Educational Background will help you identify and document information about your high school and/or college education. Start with your most recent educational accomplishments. Most college students do not need to include information about high school, but it is important to include education attained through community colleges or specialized training programs.

Part III: Educational Background will help you document:
- High School Information
- Standardized Test Scores
- Collegiate Information
- Special Academic Programs
- Certification / Ratings / Licenses
- Skills / Qualifications / Special Training

High School Information

List information about the high school you currently attend or have attended.

School Name: _____

Principal Name: _____

Guidance Counselor: _____

Address: _____

City: _____ State/Province: _____ Zip/Postal Code: _____

Telephone: _____ Fax: _____

Web Site: _____ Email: _____

Current GPA: _____ on a scale of: _____

Class Rank: _____ out of Class Size: _____

Expected Graduation Date: (Month & Year) _____

Type of School: ❏ Public   ❏ Private   ❏ Parochial   ❏ Other: _____

Previous High Schools Attended: _____

_____

Advanced Placement (AP) Courses: _____

_____

_____

Honors Courses: _____

_____

_____

College-Level Courses (List the courses you took at a community college): _____

_____

_____

Special Programs (List outside academic programs you completed, such as a summer program): _____

_____

_____

_____

Standardized Test Scores

List your test score(s) for each exam taken. Some scholarships are awarded to students based on their test scores.

SAT Scores

PSAT I Score: _____

SAT I Score: _____   Math: _____   Verbal: _____

SAT II Subject Test: _____   Score: _____

SAT II Subject Test: _____   Score: _____

SAT II Subject Test: _____   Score: _____

SAT II Subject Test: _____   Score: _____

SAT II Subject Test: _____   Score: _____

ACT Scores

Composite Score: _____   Writing: _____   Reading: _____

Reading: _____   Math: _____   Science: _____

Advanced Placement (AP) Exams

AP Exam: _____   Score: _____

AP Exam: _____   Score: _____

AP Exam: _____   Score: _____

AP Exam: _____   Score: _____

College – Level Examination Program (CLEP)

CLEP Exam: _____   Score: _____

CLEP Exam: _____   Score: _____

CLEP Exam: _____   Score: _____

CLEP Exam: _____   Score: _____

Other Exams

Exam: _____   Score: _____

Exam: _____   Score: _____

Exam: _____   Score: _____

Collegiate Information

List information about the school (i.e. college) you currently attend or have attended.

#1

Enrollment Dates　　　From:_____　　To:_____

School Name: _____

Address: _____

City:_____　　State/Province:_____　　Zip/Postal Code: _____

Telephone:_____　　Fax: _____

Web Site:_____　　Email: _____

Major: _____　　Minor: _____

Cumulative GPA: _____on a scale of: _____

Total Number of Credits Completed: _____

Degree / Certificate / License Earned: _____

Expected Graduation Date: (Month & Year) _____

Select the type of school(s) you plan to/currently attend:　(Select all that apply.)

❑ Public School
❑ Private School

❑ Trade, Technical, or Vocational School
❑ Two-year Community / Junior College
❑ Four-year College / University
❑ Graduate School
❑ Other: _____

❑ Historical Black College/University
❑ Hispanic Serving Institution
❑ Tribal School Serving the Community

Enrollment Status
You attend school:　　❑ Full-time　　❑ Part-time

Principal Courses:

_____

_____

_____

_____

_____

_____

_____

_____

_____

Collegiate Information

#2

Enrollment Dates   From:_____   To:_____

School Name: _____

Address: _____

City:_____   State/Province:_____   Zip/Postal Code: _____

Telephone:_____   Fax: _____

Web Site:_____   Email: _____

Major: _____   Minor: _____

Cumulative GPA: _____on a scale of: _____

Total Number of Credits Completed: _____

Degree / Certificate / License Earned: _____

Expected Graduation Date: (Month & Year) _____

Select the type of school(s) you plan to/currently attend: (Select all that apply.)

❑ Public School   ❑ Trade, Technical, or Vocational School   ❑ Historical Black College/University
❑ Private School   ❑ Two-year Community / Junior College   ❑ Hispanic Serving Institution
                       ❑ Four-year College / University   ❑ Tribal School Serving the Community
                       ❑ Graduate School
                       ❑ Other: _____

Enrollment Status
You attend school: ❑ Full-time   ❑ Part-time

Principal Courses:

_____

_____

_____

_____

_____

_____

_____

_____

_____

Special Academic Programs

List any special academic programs you completed such as a summer program.

	Special Program Name	Location	Dates
1.			
2.			
3.			
4.			
5.			
6.			
7.			
8.			
9.			
10.			

Certification / Ratings / Licenses

List all of your certificates, ratings, and/or licenses, and the dates you received them. Examples: Private Pilot Certificate - 5/03/97, Lifeguard - 8/1/01, Cardio-Pulmonary Resuscitation (CPR) Certification - 11/12/00

	Certification / Ratings / Licenses	Date
1.		
2.		
3.		
4.		
5.		
6.		
7.		
8.		
9.		
10.		
11.		
12.		

Skills / Qualifications / Special Training

List all of your skills, qualifications, and/or special training you received, include dates. Examples:
Computer Programmer, Typing Speed, etc.

Skill / Qualifications / Special Training   Date

1. _____
2. _____
3. _____
4. _____
5. _____
6. _____
7. _____
8. _____
9. _____
10. _____

Additional Notes

_____
_____
_____
_____
_____
_____
_____
_____
_____
_____
_____
_____
_____
_____
_____

Part IV
Work Experiences

Part IV: Work Experiences will help you identify and document information about all work experiences, including part-time, summer, freelance and voluntary work. Your participation in any research projects, internships, and cooperative education programs should also be listed as work experiences. Start with your most recent employer. This information will also help you create a scholarship and job resume.

Need Help Describing Your Job Responsibilities
Describe your job responsibilities using verb phrases. In order to explain your job responsibilities, pretend you are telling someone about your job. Beginning each sentence with "I… "

For example:
- "I mentored high school students in math."
- "I designed posters for the football team."

Whenever you are ready to create your resume, use the information provided below. Delete the "I" and use the remaining verb phrase to describe your job responsibilities:
- "Mentored high school students in math."
- "Designed posters for the football team"

Use present tense verbs for your present job(s), and past tense verbs for past jobs. If you need help finding the right verbs to use, review the list of verb tenses on the next page to assist you with explaining your job responsibilities.

Action Verbs For Describing Your Job Responsibilities

If you have difficulty finding the right verbs to describe your job responsibilities, choose from the following list:

Accomplished	Created	Indoctrinated	Reconciled
Achieved	Critiqued	Influenced	Recorded
Acquired	Cut	Informed	Recruited
Acted	Decreased	Initiated	Reduced
Adapted	Delegated	Innovated	Referred
Addressed	Decided	Inspected	Regulated
Adjusted	Defined	Instructed	Rehabilitated
Administered	Delivered	Insured	Related
Advanced	Demonstrated	Integrated	Remodeled
Advised	Determined	Interpreted	Repaired
Allocated	Designed	Interviewed	Reported
Analyzed	Developed	Introduced	Represented
Applied	Devised	Invented	Researched
Appraised	Diagnosed	Investigated	Restored
Approved	Directed	Kept	Restructured
Arranged	Dispatched	Launched	Retrieved
Assembled	Distinguished	Lectured	Reversed
Assigned	Distributed	Led	Reviewed
Assisted	Diversified	Made	Revised
Attained	Drafted	Maintained	Revitalized
Audited	Edited	Managed	Saved
Author	Educated	Manufactured	Scheduled
Automated	Eliminated	Marketed	Schooled
Balanced	Enabled	Mediated	Screened
Brought	Encouraged	Moderated	Selected
Budgeted	Engineered	Modified	Serviced
Built	Enlisted	Monitored	Set
Calculated	Established	Motivated	Shaped
Catalogued	Ensured	Negotiated	Screened
Chaired	Estimated	Observed	Selected
Changed	Evaluated	Operated	Simplified
Clarified	Examined	Ordered	Skilled
Coached	Executed	Organized	Sold
Collected	Expanded	Originated	Solidified
Communicated	Expedited	Outsold	Solved
Compared	Extracted	Overhauled	Specified
Compiled	Fabricated	Oversaw	Stimulated
Completed	Facilitated	Participated	Streamlined
Composed	Familiarized	Performed	Strengthened
Computed	Fashioned	Persuaded	Suggested
Computerized	Finalized	Planned	Summarized
Conceptualized	Focused	Prepared	Supervised
Conceived	Forecast	Presented	Surveyed
Concluded	Formulated	Presided	Systemized
Conducted	Founded	Prioritized	Tabulated
Conserved	Gathered	Processed	Taught
Consolidated	Generated	Produced	Tested
Contained	Graded	Programmed	Trained
Continued	Guided	Projected	Translated
Contracted	Handled	Promoted	Traveled
Contributed	Headed Up	Proposed	Trimmed
Controlled	Identified	Provided	Updated
Coordinated	Illustrated	Publicized	Upgraded
Corrected	Implemented	Published	Validated
Corresponded	Improved	Purchased	Worked
Counseled	Increased	Recommended	Wrote

Work Experiences

List all of your work experiences.

#1

Employment Dates   Start:_____   End: _____

Job Position/Title:_____   Pay Rate / Salary: _____

Supervisor: _____

Company Name:_____

Address: _____

City: _____   State/Province: _____   Zip/Postal Code: _____

Telephone: _____   Fax: _____

Web Site: _____   Email: _____

Job Responsibilities:

I _____

I _____

I _____

I _____

#2

Employment Dates   Start:_____   End: _____

Job Position/Title:_____   Pay Rate / Salary: _____

Supervisor: _____

Company Name:_____

Address: _____

City: _____   State/Province: _____   Zip/Postal Code: _____

Telephone: _____   Fax: _____

Web Site: _____   Email: _____

Job Responsibilities:

I _____

I _____

I _____

I _____

#3

Employment Dates   Start:_____   End: _____

Job Position/Title:_____   Pay Rate / Salary: _____

Supervisor: _____

Company Name:_____

Address: _____

City: _____   State/Province: _____   Zip/Postal Code: _____

Telephone: _____   Fax: _____

Web Site: _____   Email: _____

Job Responsibilities:

I _____

I _____

I _____

I _____

#4

Employment Dates   Start:_____   End: _____

Job Position/Title:_____   Pay Rate / Salary: _____

Supervisor: _____

Company Name:_____

Address: _____

City: _____   State/Province: _____   Zip/Postal Code: _____

Telephone: _____   Fax: _____

Web Site: _____   Email: _____

Job Responsibilities:

I _____

I _____

I _____

I _____

Volunteer or Research Experiences

List all of your volunteer and research experiences.

#1

Volunteer Dates   Start:_____   End: _____

Job Position/Title:_____   Pay Rate / Salary: _____

Supervisor: _____

Organization Name: _____

Address: _____

City: _____   State/Province: _____   Zip/Postal Code: _____

Telephone: _____   Fax: _____

Web Site: _____   Email: _____

Job Responsibilities:

I _____

I _____

I _____

I _____

#2

Volunteer Dates   Start:_____   End: _____

Job Position/Title:_____   Pay Rate / Salary: _____

Supervisor: _____

Organization Name: _____

Address: _____

City: _____   State/Province: _____   Zip/Postal Code: _____

Telephone: _____   Fax: _____

Web Site: _____   Email: _____

Job Responsibilities:

I _____

I _____

I _____

I _____

#3

Volunteer Dates   Start:_____   End: _____

Job Position/Title:_____   Pay Rate / Salary: _____

Supervisor: _____

Organization Name: _____

Address: _____

City: _____   State/Province: _____   Zip/Postal Code: _____

Telephone: _____   Fax: _____

Web Site: _____   Email: _____

Job Responsibilities:

I _____

I _____

I _____

I _____

#4

Volunteer Dates   Start:_____   End: _____

Job Position/Title:_____   Pay Rate / Salary: _____

Supervisor: _____

Organization Name: _____

Address: _____

City: _____   State/Province: _____   Zip/Postal Code: _____

Telephone: _____   Fax: _____

Web Site: _____   Email: _____

Job Responsibilities:

I _____

I _____

I _____

I _____

Professional Training Programs

List all professional training programs you have attended.

Professional Training Program	Location	Dates
1.		
2.		
3.		
4.		
5.		
6.		
7.		
8.		
9.		
10.		

Additional Notes

_____

_____

_____

_____

_____

_____

_____

_____

_____

_____

_____

_____

_____

_____

_____

_____

_____

Part V
Extracurricular Activities

Part V: Extracurricular Activities will help you identify and document information about your extracurricular activities. Extracurricular activities are great ways to become a well-rounded individual and improve your chances of winning a scholarship.

Part V: Extracurricular Activities will help you identify and document:
- Leadership Positions
- School Involvement
- Community Involvement
- Honors and Awards
- Seminars/Conferences/Workshops
- Artistic Talents
- Athletic Talents
- Interests/Hobbies
- Travel Experiences

Leadership Positions

List all the organizations that you were/are an active member, include any positions held and the year(s) you were a participant. High school activities may be included if you are currently a high school student or college freshman. Examples: Alpha Eta Rho - President 2000, Tennis Team – Captain 2001

	Organization's Name	Position	Date
1.			
2.			
3.			
4.			
5.			
6.			
7.			
8.			
9.			
10.			

School Involvement

List all of your school activities, in which you have participated during your enrollment in school. Begin with your most recent involvement(s). Example: student council, clubs, sports team, interest groups, peer tutoring, school volunteer experiences, graduation committee, etc.

	Organization's Name	Position	Date
1.			
2.			
3.			
4.			
5.			
6.			
7.			
8.			
9.			
10.			

Community Involvement

Select or list all of your volunteer activities relating to your community (outside of school) such as tutoring kids, church groups, choirs, etc. Start with your most recent community involvement(s).

- ❑ Animals
- ❑ Arts & Culture
- ❑ Children & Youth Organizations
- ❑ Crisis, Emergency & Safety Services
- ❑ Disabled/Special Needs Persons
- ❑ Education & Literacy Projects
- ❑ Environmental/Beautification Projects

- ❑ Health & Medical Related Organizations
- ❑ Homeless & Hunger Relief
- ❑ Housing/Habitat & Building Projects
- ❑ Race & Ethnicity
- ❑ Religion/Faith-Based Organizations
- ❑ Seniors/Elderly Organizations
- ❑ Sports & Recreation

Other:_____

_____

_____

_____

_____

_____

_____

Honors & Awards

List all your scholastic, extracurricular, and civic honors and awards, include the dates. Start with the most recent honors and awards. If there is more than one honors or awards in a given year, list the most significant one first. If some honors and awards span several years (e.g. Honor Roll Standing 2001- 03), put the longest term first. Examples: Kodak Award, Dean's List, National Honor Society, etc.

                             Honors and Awards   Date

1. _____

2. _____

3. _____

4. _____

5. _____

6. _____

7. _____

8. _____

9. _____

10. _____

Seminars/Conferences/Workshops

List all seminars, conferences, and workshops you attended such as basketball workshops, leadership retreats, crisis training, etc. You should include the event, place, and date. Begin with the most recent. Example: Healthy Schools Conference, Victoria, IL 2005

	Event	Place	Date
1.			
2.			
3.			
4.			
5.			
6.			
7.			
8.			
9.			
10.			
11.			
12.			

Artistic Talents and Achievements

Select or list all of your artistic talents and achievements. Start with your most recent achievements (i.e. Best Performance, First Solo, etc.).

❑ Cinematography
❑ Dance
❑ Literary Composition
❑ Musical Instrument: _____
❑ Oratory

❑ Painting
❑ Photography
❑ Sculpting
❑ Theater
❑ Vocal Musician

Other:_____

_____

_____

_____

_____

_____

_____

Athletic Talents and Achievements

Select or list all of your athletic talents and achievements. Start with your most recent achievements. Include your participation in solo and team events, MVP awards, etc.

- ❑ Alpine/Nordic Skiing
- ❑ Archery
- ❑ Baseball/Softball
- ❑ Basketball
- ❑ Bowling
- ❑ Boxing
- ❑ Cycling
- ❑ Equestrian/Polo

- ❑ Fencing
- ❑ Field Hockey
- ❑ Football
- ❑ Golf
- ❑ Gymnastics
- ❑ Ice Hockey
- ❑ Lacrosse
- ❑ Martial Arts

- ❑ Racquet/Court
- ❑ Sports
- ❑ Rodeo
- ❑ Rugby
- ❑ Sailing/Rowing
- ❑ Soccer
- ❑ Swimming/Diving
- ❑ Skating

- ❑ Table Tennis
- ❑ Track and Field
- ❑ Water Skiing
- ❑ Weight Lifting
- ❑ Wrestling
- ❑ Volleyball

Other:_____

_____

_____

_____

_____

_____

_____

Interests/Hobbies

List your interests/hobbies and other activities done alone and with others that gives you enjoyment.

_____

_____

_____

_____

_____

_____

_____

_____

_____

_____

_____

_____

Travel Experiences

List your travel experiences and what you learned from them.

_____
_____
_____
_____
_____
_____
_____
_____
_____
_____
_____
_____
_____

Additional Notes

_____
_____
_____
_____
_____
_____
_____
_____
_____
_____
_____
_____
_____
_____
_____

Part VI
References

Part VI: References will help you list the names and addresses of individuals you would use as a reference and/or to write a letter of recommendation. References are used to form an idea of what others think about you. A good reference is someone who knows you well. He/she should be able to answer questions about your character, academics, leadership, teamwork, and/or extracurricular activities. Select your references carefully.

Who to Ask to Write a Letter of Recommendation

It is important that you ask the right people to write a good letter of recommendation for you. You should ask people who have known you in different situations (i.e. job supervisor, professor, coach, religious leaders, etc.) so they may speak about your various qualities. A diverse group of letters of recommendation can create a broader and more accurate picture of you as a person. Unfortunately, your parents and other family members cannot write a letter of recommendation. Before you list someone as a reference, make sure you have that person's permission to do so.

In general, the best letters of recommendation are from people who:
- Have worked with you closely (i.e. teacher, coach, supervisor)
- Have known you long enough to write with authority (i.e. academic advisor)
- Are well known (i.e. a departmental chair, head coach, principal, religious leader)
- Have a positive opinion of you and your abilities

If you are not sure whether prospective references know you well or have a positive impression of you to write a good letter, there is nothing wrong with asking them whether they would be able to write a good letter. After all, if you are going to compete with other applicants who have excellent references and glowing letters of recommendation, a bland or somewhat positive letter of recommendation from someone who doesn't really know you, can actually do more harm than good.

Advice

Once you have 3-4 references that are willing to write letters of recommendation for you, there are several things you can do to increase your chances of receiving glowing letters of recommendation:

- **Start Early**
  Give your references plenty of time to write a good letter of recommendation. If you are going to ask a teacher or someone at school, you must ask them early, since their schedule gets busier throughout the school year. Make sure you give your references as much time as possible before the application deadline. A minimum of three or four weeks is customary and will allow you to check back a week before the deadline to ensure that the letter of recommendation was completed and has been sent to the scholarship provider according to their guidelines. In some cases, references may request that you write the first draft.

- **Recommendation Track Form**
  The Recommendation Track Form, located in Part VIII, will help you and the references writing your letters of recommendations organize this process. Use this form for each individual that writes a letter of recommendation for you.

- **Scholarship Details**
  Give each reference information about the organization awarding the scholarship, the scholarship's purpose, guidelines, eligibility requirements, deadline, and specific instructions (if any) regarding the letter of recommendation.

- **Give Your Input**
  You can help your references create good letters of recommendation by providing them with useful information about yourself, especially if you have not worked or spoken to them for several months or possibly years. This information will also refresh their memories with details about your goals, skills, work habits, and achievements. A good letter of recommendation should not be longer than two pages in length.

  References often find the following information helpful when writing letters of recommendation:
  - Details about the scholarship(s)
  - Your College Plans (if necessary)
  - Scholarship Resume
  - List of Achievement, Awards, and Honors
  - List of Extracurricular Activities (inside and outside of school)

  Advice: You should give your references copies of certain parts of your workbook such as **Part V: Extracurricular Activities**.

- **Provide a Stamped Envelope**
  If the letter should be mailed directly to the scholarship provider, you should provide a stamped envelope addressed to the scholarship provider. If the letter should be returned to you in a sealed envelope, be sure to print/type your name and address and the scholarship's name on the outside of the envelope.

- **Forms**
  Some scholarship providers may have a recommendation form for your references to complete. Recommendation forms typically ask questions about your character, academics, leadership, teamwork, leadership, and/or extracurricular activities.

- **Request a Copy of the Letter**
  Ask your references to make a copy of the letter of recommendation for your records. You may be able to use the same letter of recommendation for other scholarship application, except your references will have to revise it by changing the date, the scholarship name, and certain information within the letter to tailor it for the specific scholarship.

- **Send a thank you note**
  You should send your references a thank you note or card for taking the time to write the letters of recommendation for you.

References

List information about the individuals you want to use as references or to write a letter of recommendation.

#1

Name: _____ Relationship: _____

Occupation: _____

Address: _____

_____

City: _____ State/Province: _____ Zip/Postal Code: _____

Telephone: _____ Email: _____

#2

Name: _____ Relationship: _____

Occupation: _____

Address: _____

_____

City: _____ State/Province: _____ Zip/Postal Code: _____

Telephone: _____ Email: _____

#3

Name: _____ Relationship: _____

Occupation: _____

Address: _____

_____

City: _____ State/Province: _____ Zip/Postal Code: _____

Telephone: _____ Email: _____

#4

Name: _____ Relationship: _____

Occupation: _____

Address: _____

_____

City: _____ State/Province: _____ Zip/Postal Code: _____

Telephone: _____ Email: _____

#5

Name: _____ Relationship: _____

Occupation: _____

Address: _____

_____

City: _____ State/Province: _____ Zip/Postal Code: _____

Telephone: _____ Email: _____

#6

Name: _____ Relationship: _____

Occupation: _____

Address: _____

_____

City: _____ State/Province: _____ Zip/Postal Code: _____

Telephone: _____ Email: _____

#7

Name: _____ Relationship: _____

Occupation: _____

Address: _____

_____

City: _____ State/Province: _____ Zip/Postal Code: _____

Telephone: _____ Email: _____

#8

Name: _____ Relationship: _____

Occupation: _____

Address: _____

_____

City: _____ State/Province: _____ Zip/Postal Code: _____

Telephone: _____ Email: _____

Creating a Reference List

The design of your reference list should be consistent with your resume. You should use the same heading, fonts, and general layout. Be sure to ask permission before including someone on your reference list. Usually, a reference list consists of at least two references. Always carry a copy of your resume and reference list to an interview.

List your references:
- Names
- Titles
- Employers (if applicable)
- Addresses
- Phone Numbers
- Email Addresses

Example:

John Doe
Professor
AvScholars University
1234 North Ave
Chicago, IL 60610
(123) 123-456-7894
hdoe@avscholars-university.edu

Sample Reference List is available on the next page.

John Doe
1234 N. LaSalle Ave
Atlanta, GA   123456
(123) 123-4567 Home
(123) 987-6543 Cell
johndoe@sampleresume.com

Reference List

Anne Lee
Supervisor
XYZ Electronics, Inc.
361 Company Way
Atlanta, GA 12345
(123) 82x-xxxx
annelee@xyz.com

Tedd Sawyson
Professor
Economics Department
North University
Chicago, IL 98765
(987) 75x-xxxx
tsawyson@nu.edu

James Williams
Team Leader
Volunteer Food Shelter
1234 New Ave
Chicago, IL 98765
(987) 92x-xxxx
jamesw@foodshelter.com

Mike Jenkins
Coach – Track Team
North University
Chicago, IL 98765
(987) 75x-xxxx
coachjenkins@nu.edu

Sample
Reference List

Part VII
Resume Template

Part VII: Resume Template will help you create a scholarship resume. Refer to other parts of this workbook to help you complete the resume template. A sample scholarship resume is provided for your review.

Creating a Scholarship Resume

A scholarship resume is your SALES TOOL. It is slightly different than a job resume. The major focus of a scholarship resume is your education, extracurricular activities, achievements, awards, and honors. A job resume basically focuses on your work experiences and skills. Do not use a job resume when applying for a scholarship.

Your scholarship resume should be tailored to the type of scholarship for which you are applying. Remember, your resume should be detailed enough to provide the scholarship committee with specific information to assess your qualifications. The scholarship committee will SKIM, not read, your resume. Your resume needs to be concise and contain only pertinent information that will get the scholarship committee's attention.

The main components of a scholarship resume include:
- **Contact Information**
  Your name, address (present and/or permanent), phone number(s), and email address.
- **Career Objective**
  Use a single phase expressing your career goals
- **Education**
  List the schools you have attended and expected graduation date, major, and G.P.A. Start with your most recent school enrollment.
- **Achievements, Awards and Honors**
  List your academic, artistic, and/or athletic achievements, honors, and awards. Start with your most recent achievements, honors, and awards.
- **Extracurricular Activities**
  List your extracurricular activities inside and outside of school such as: leadership positions, school involvement, community involvement, etc. Start with your most recent activities.
- **Work Experiences** (if space permits)
  List your work experiences. Volunteer, research projects, internships, and cooperative education programs that you experienced should also be listed as work experiences. Start with your most recent work experience and give the dates of employment, the employer's name, job title, and job responsibilities.

DO NOT INCLUDE
- Personal Data
  Do not list personal data such as height, weight, sex, and marital status on your resume. This information is irrelevant.
- References
  Do not list your references on the resume. Instead, use the phrase "References Available on Request," if you have enough space at the bottom of your resume.

Editing Your Resume
- Eliminate data that falls into the "padding" or "exaggeration" category.
- Be concise and clear.
- Do not include any negative information.

<u>Resume Format</u>
- Keep it to one page (if possible).
- Do not use more than 2 different types of fonts and use font size 12 points for the main text.
- Use bullets or bold fonts to highlight significant information.
- SPELL CHECK and PROOF READ your resume more than once!
- Have someone else proof read your resume.
- Use good quality paper such as white or neutral colored paper.

Additional Resources

If you have access to a computer, most word processing programs have a resume template that you can use, or you can consult various books on resume writing at your local library. The Internet also has numerous resume writing web sites, in which some companies charge a fee for their services.

Scholarship Resume Template

Name:_____

Address:_____

City: _____   State: _____   Zip/Postal Code: _____

Telephone_____

Email: _____

Career Objective
Use a single phase expressing your career goals

_____

_____

Education
List the school(s) you currently attend and have attended. You should document information about your expected graduation date, major, and G.P.A. Start with your most recent school enrollment.

School Name:_____

Major/Minor: _____

Expected Graduation Date: (Month & Year) _____

Cumulative GPA: _____ / _____ (GPA Scale)

School Name:_____

Major/Minor: _____

Expected Graduation Date: (Month & Year) _____

Cumulative GPA: _____ / _____ (GPA Scale)

Extracurricular Activities
List your extracurricular activities inside and outside of school such as: leadership positions, school involvement, community involvement, etc. Start with your most recent activities.

Year(s)	Organization's Name	Status (i.e. member, President)

Awards and Honors

List your academic and/or athletic achievements, honors, and awards. Start with your most recent achievements, honors, and awards.

Year(s)   Award's Name

_____

_____

_____

_____

_____

_____

_____

Skills and Special Training

List your skills, special training, or spoken languages.

_____

_____

_____

_____

_____

_____

_____

_____

Work Experience (if space permits)

List your work experiences. Volunteer, research projects, internships, and cooperative education programs that you experienced should also be listed as work experiences. Start with your most recent employer and give the dates of employment, the employer's name, job title, and job responsibilities.

Employment Dates   Job Title
                        Company Name
                        • Job Responsibilities
                        • Job Responsibilities

_____ to _____   _____

                        _____

                    •   _____

                    •   _____

_____ to _____   _____

                        _____

                    •   _____

                    •   _____

_____ to _____   _____

                        _____

                    •   _____

                    •   _____

References Available on Request (if space permits)

John Doe
1234 N. LaSalle Ave
Atlanta, GA   123456
(123) 123-4567 Home
(123) 987-6543 Alternate Number
johndoe@sampleresume.com

Career Objective

To obtain a Bachelor of Science Degree in Aviation and become a Professional Airline Pilot

Education

August 2000 to Present	Chicago High School
	Computer Technology
	Expected Graduation: June 2004
	GPA: 3.4/4.0

Extracurricular Activities

2003	Guest Speaker for Career Day at Woodward Elementary School
2001 - Present	Founder and President, ACES of STEPHENSON HIGH FLYING JAGS
2002 - 2003	Volunteer Mentor for MLK High School Aviation Club
1999 - Present	Civil Air Patrol, Peachtree Dekalb Airport, SER GA 065
2001 - 2002	Defensive Tackle for the Redan Park Football Team
2000 - 2002	Stephenson High Marching Band

Awards and Honors

2001 - Present	National Honor Society
2000 - Present	Honor Role Student
2002	Interview on CNN with Lt. Colonel Charles Dryden, Original Tuskegee Airman
2001	Student Ambassador to Australia and New Zealand for 2002
2001	WHO's WHO among American High School Students 2001

Skills and Special Training

2002	Private Pilot Certificate
2001	CPR Certificate

Work Experiences

May 2002 to Present	Cashier
	Jobs 'R Us, Chicago, IL
	• Perform cashier duties
September 1999 to April 2000	Volunteer Math Tutor
	Kid Smarts, Atlanta, GA
	• Volunteered as a math tutor to students in 5th grade

References Available on Request

Part VIII
Track Forms

There are three track forms designed to keep your stress level to a minimum by assisting you with each phase of your scholarship search and the application process.

- **Scholarship Track Form**
  The Scholarship Track Form will help you keep track of your scholarship searches, important dates, and to make sure that you send all the supporting documents requested by the scholarship provider along with your application. Use this form for each scholarship you're applying to as an applicant and before mailing your application to the scholarship provider.

- **Interview Track Form**
  The Interview Track Form will help you prepare for the scholarship interview and keep track of your interview date, location, and time. Use this form for each scholarship interview.

- **Recommendation Track Form**
  The Recommendation Track Form will help you and your references organize this process. Use this form for each individual that will write a letter recommendation for you.

Scholarship Track Form

Scholarship's Name: _____

Organization's Name: _____

Contact Person: _____

Address: _____

City: _____ State/Province: _____ Zip/Postal Code: _____

Tel.: _____ Fax: _____

Email: _____ Web Site: _____

Award Source: (i.e. employer) _____ Award Amount: _____

Type of Award:
❏ Scholarship
❏ Grant
❏ Fellowship

Scholarship Category:
❏ National Award
❏ Regional Award
❏ State Award
❏ Local Award
❏ Institutional Award
❏ International Award

Renewable:
❏ Yes
❏ No

Important Dates

Request Letter Sent: _____ Application Mailed: _____

Application Received: _____ Scholarship Deadline Date: _____

Application Completed: _____

Supporting Documents Required:
This section help you send all the appropriate information requested by the scholarship provider. Select all the checkboxes that applies to the scholarship application before mailing it to the scholarship provider.

❏ Resume
❏ Academic Transcript(s)
❏ Letters of Recommendations
❏ Essay/Personal Statement
❏ Copies of Certificates, Licenses, or Ratings
❏ Reference List
❏ Sample of Work / Portfolio
❏ Sample of Artwork or Performances

❏ Photograph
❏ Copy of Federal Income Tax Information
❏ Self-Addressed, Stamped Envelope
❏ Other: _____

❏ **Make a copy of entire package for your file**

Notes:

_____

_____

_____

Results: ❏ I Won!   ❏ Reapply Next Year

Interview Track Form

Award Name: _____

Sponsoring Organization: _____

Contact Person: _____

Address: _____

City: _____ State/Province: _____ Zip/Postal Code: _____

Tel.: _____ Fax: _____

Email: _____ Web Site: _____

Award Source: (i.e. employer) _____ Award Amount: _____

Interview Checklist:
- ❏ Copy of complete Application Packet
- ❏ Recommendations
- ❏ Essay
- ❏ Reference List
- ❏ Copy of Federal Income Tax return
- ❏ Scholarship Resume
- ❏ Audiotape of performance
- ❏ Photograph
- ❏ Other: _____

Personal Checklist:
- ❏ Suit Dry Cleaned / Ironed
- ❏ Shoes Polished
- ❏ Hair Cut
- ❏ No earrings for males

Review Scholarship Materials
- ❏ Purpose, Objectives, Goals
- ❏ Thank You Letter for Interview

Interview Information

Interview Date: _____ Location: _____ Time: _____

Notes:

_____

_____

_____

_____

_____

_____

_____

_____

_____

_____

Recommendation Track Form

Reference Name: _____   Tel.: _____

Recommendation For

Name: _____

Address: _____

City: _____   State/Province: _____   Zip/Postal Code: _____

Tel.: _____   Fax: _____

Email: _____   Web Site: _____

Send Recommendation To: ❑ **Student will pick up recommendation letter**

Award Name: _____

Sponsoring Organization: _____

Contact Person: _____

Address: _____

City: _____   State/Province: _____   Zip/Postal Code: _____

Important Dates: **Documents Enclosed:** (Select all that applies)
❑ Parts of Scholarship Worksheet
Scholarship Deadline Date: _____   ❑ Scholarship Resume
❑ Scholarship Guidelines and Details
Recommendation Completed: _____   ❑ Self-Addressed, Stamped Envelope
❑ Recommendation Form
Recommendation Mailed: _____   ❑ Other: _____

Notes:

_____

_____

_____

_____

_____

_____

❑ **Make a copy of the recommendation letter for your records**

Chapter 3
Scholarship & Financial Aid Sources

There are various scholarship and financial aid sources that can assist you with paying for your post-secondary education (i.e. college, vocational school, etc.). You need to create a clear plan, an outline, of the sources that are available to you. Increase your odds of actually winning a scholarship by starting locally and expanding outward, since many scholarships come from local businesses, private foundations, and community organizations.

The Fall season is the best time to start your scholarship search, since many businesses and organizations send announcements and applications to newspapers, magazines, high school teachers, and guidance counselors at the being of the school year. You should ask any and everyone about possible scholarship opportunities to assist you with paying for school. Being persistent will pay-off.

Scholarship and financial aid sources consist of:

- Parents & Students
- Financial Aid Workshops
- High School Resources
- College Resources
- Institutional Aid
- Federal Programs
- State Education Agencies
- Private Lenders
- College Savings Plans
- Education Tax Credits
- Military Education Benefits
- Libraries and Librarians
- SAT & ACT Exams
- Internet Scholarship Search Directories
- Banks / Credit Unions
- Employers
- Volunteer - Make a Difference
- Public Officials
- Organization, Associations, Unions
- Chamber of Commerce
- Conventions / Trade Shows / Conferences
- Scholarship & College Directories
- Magazines
- Newspapers
- Churches/Religious Organizations
- Internships / Co-Op Programs
- Financial Planners

Now that you have reviewed this list, lets explore them in more details.

Parents & Students

Your parents are considered your primary source of paying for your college education. Parents should plan ahead by developing a savings strategy once their child is born or while attending elementary school. It's never too late for parents to start saving for their child's college education. As a parent, there are various sources you should consider to help pay for your child's education such as 529 College Savings Plans.

Students are also expected to help pay for their college education. Since, you are expected to provide some funding, there are a few savings strategies you should consider such as saving a certain percentage of your allowance or employment checks. Once you have started your savings plan, you should discuss with your parent(s) and consider depositing your money into a bank account that would provide you with the highest return on your money (interest). An example would be a Money Market Account, which offers compounding interest on a monthly or quarterly basis. You should research the different banking institutions in your city to learn more about other savings strategies and types of bank accounts.

Financial Aid Workshops

Many high schools, colleges, and organizations (i.e. state education agencies, banks, lenders) sponsor financial aid workshops to help high school students and their parents gain a better understanding about the college admission and financial aid process. These workshops typically take place during the months of November through February. Most workshops are offered free of charge to the public. Be aware that some organizations charge a fee for families to attend their workshops and to perform scholarship searches, but you can obtain the same information from free financial aid workshops or scholarship search web sites.

Financial aid workshops typically provide families with information on:
- The college admission and financial aid process.
- How financial aid eligibility is determined.
- How to fill out the Free Application for Federal Student Aid (FAFSA) and other relevant forms.
- Various sources of financial aid.

Financial aid workshops allow families to complete their FAFSA with financial aid professionals on-hand to answer individual questions. Because the FAFSA require specific financial information, participants may be asked to bring the following items to the workshop: Federal and State 1040 Tax returns for parents and students (if possible); W-2 Forms for parents and students; and Untaxed Income Amounts (i.e. AADC, SSI, Child Support, etc.). To expedite the process, families should complete the FAFSA as much as possible in advance before attending a financial aid workshop. For additional information about financial aid workshops scheduled in your city, you should ask your high school guidance counselors and teachers.

High School Resources

Many students do not use all the available resources at their high school. Your principle, guidance counselors, teachers, faculty, staff, and coaches are all part of a "networking center" to help their students. Some high schools offer scholarships to their students continuing their education. The following resources are available at your high school:

- Guidance Counselors
  Guidance counselors are excellent resources to ask about scholarship information. They are in contact with local businesses, private foundations, and community organizations that may offer scholarships to students. Guidance counselors assist students on a daily basis, and their job is to provide you and your parent(s) with some form of guidance to assist you with your educational and career goals. Guidance counselors are typically helping numerous students and parents, and they may not have time to contact you on a weekly basis. To avoid missing out on some "golden" scholarship opportunities, you should visit your guidance counselor(s) at least once a week to inquire about any scholarships.

- Teachers / Coaches / Faculty
  Students searching for scholarships often overlook teachers, coaches, faculty, and staff members. These administrators may be aware of some scholarships offered by their professional organizations, local businesses, and/or clubs.

- School Library
  Your school's library should have some books and magazines on the subject of financial aid. These books are located in the reference section of the library. Your school's librarian may be aware of some local scholarships for students. Don't hesitate to ask.

- Students
  Ask fellow students that are continuing their education about any scholarship(s) they have applied to as an applicant or heard about from someone else. Some students may be hesitant to tell you about their scholarship opportunities, since you may be competing against them.

- Clubs & Organizations
  If you are a member of a club or organization at your school, you should ask the organization's advisor or president about possible scholarships for members. If your club/organization is one of many chapters, you should contact the national and regional offices to inquire about scholarship opportunities for members. It's best to ask the secretary or receptionist, since most announcements are filtered through their desk, or they can forward your call to the appropriate person(s) or department.

- School Newspaper / Newsletters
  Some local and community scholarships may be announced in your school's newspaper or newsletters.

- Bulletin Boards
  Information about scholarships may be posted on the bulletin boards in your school's main office, counselor's office, near the lunchroom, or other high traffic areas where students filter through the halls. Whenever you are walking through the halls of your school, you should take a glance at the bulletin boards for scholarship information.

College Resources

Many students do not use all the available resources at their school. Your professors, counselors, teachers, faculty, staff, and coaches are all part of a "networking center" to help their students. The following resources are available at your high school:

- College Web Sites
  Visit the web site of the school(s) you plan to/currently attend. Most schools post information about their financial aid programs and scholarships on their web site. You should browse the following areas on each school's web site: admissions, financial aid, academic departments, clubs & organizations, school sponsored awards, etc.

- The Financial Aid Office (FAO) and Administrators
  The financial aid office administers and oversees how financial aid is allocated to their school's students. Within each financial aid office, there is a staff of financial aid administrators to help you and your parent(s) understand the entire financial aid process.   The financial aid administrators are your best resources about financial aid programs and application procedures, especially at that particular school. If you have any questions, you should not hesitate to call and talk to an administrator about your questions. Their service is FREE.

  The school's financial aid office may have additional information about scholarships sponsored by alumni and private organizations designated for students attending their school. There may be several binders with a listing of scholarships, a computerized database, and/or a bulletin board with posted scholarship information within the financial aid office.

- Career Center / Placement Office
  Most schools have a career center/placement office for their students. The purpose of a career center/placement office is to inform their school's students about internships, cooperative education programs, and job opportunities. Visit your school's career center/placement office, and ask the staff about any scholarships and internship opportunities for students in your career field. Some scholarship and internship opportunities may be posted on the bulletin boards within their office. There may be several binders and/or a computerized database listing scholarship, internship, and job opportunities within the career center.

- Professors / Coaches / Faculty Members
  Students searching for scholarships often overlook professors, coaches, faculty, and staff members. These administrators may be aware of some scholarships specifically for your major offered by industry businesses or organizations. These administrators are in contact with various organizations and businesses that may offer scholarships and internship opportunities, or they may know of another scholarship provider to refer you. Some academic departments offer their own scholarships, in which the financial aid office may not be informed about their departmental scholarships.

- Alumni Associations
  Most schools have an alumni association in which its members give generous donations to help provide scholarships to students attending their school. In order to be eligible for these scholarships, you must also meet other eligibility requirements. You should ask your academic advisor and visit your school's alumni affairs office and/or student affairs office (if applicable) to inquire about possible scholarships.

- Cultural and Religious Centers
  Most schools have cultural and religious centers for students of various ethnic and religious backgrounds to relax and gather with their peers. If you are apart of a particular ethnic or religious group, visit your school's cultural and/or religious centers and inquire about any scholarship opportunities. Ask the director or receptionist, if the cultural or religious center offer scholarships or know of any organizations that offer scholarships to students.

- Students
  Ask fellow students, if they heard of any scholarship announcements or applied to any scholarships in previous years. Some students may be hesitant to tell you about their scholarship opportunities, since you may be competing against them.

- Fraternities and Sororities
  Many fraternities and sororities offer scholarships to its members and non-members. Contact the fraternities and sororities at your school for more information. You should also contact the organization's national headquarters and regional offices for scholarship information.

- Clubs / Organizations
  If you are a member of a club/organization at your school, you should ask the organization's advisor or president about possible scholarships for members. If your club/organization is one of many chapters, you should contact the national and regional offices and inquire about scholarship opportunities for members. It's best to ask the secretary or receptionist, since most announcements are filtered through their desk, or they can forward your call to the appropriate person(s) or department.

- School Newspaper
  Some local, community, and national scholarships are announced in your school's newspaper.

- Bulletin Boards
  Information about scholarships and internships may be posted on the bulletin boards on-campus (i.e. academic department's main office, dean's office, main entrance to the building, or other high traffic areas on campus). Whenever you are walking through the halls of your school's buildings on-campus, you should take a glance at the bulletin boards for scholarship and internship information.

Institutional Aid

Most schools offer Institutional Aid to eligible students. Usually, Institutional Aid is awarded on a first-come, first-serve basis. You should contact the financial aid office of the school(s) you plan to or currently attend, and request a financial aid guide detailing their school's Institutional Aid and eligibility requirements. This information may be posted on the school's web site.

In addition to the FAFSA, your school may require you to complete additional forms to determine your eligibility for their Institutional Aid. You should complete and submit all required forms by the deadline date for Institutional Aid. If you do not submit the required form(s) by the deadline, you risk not receiving aid or receiving reduced aid from your school. Institutional Aid may vary from year to year.

Provided below is a list of various Institutional Aid programs offered by some schools:
- Academic Scholarships
- Departmental Scholarships
- Endowed Scholarship Funds
- Sport Scholarships
- Fee Remissions
- Prepayment Plans
- Discounts for Alumni Children and Student Leaders
- Recruitment Scholarships or Discounts
- Tuition Equalization
- Emergency Loan Programs
- Installment & Deferred Payment Plans
- Employee Discount Programs
- Financial Aid for Returning Adults
- Financial Aid for International Students
- Financial Aid for Graduate & Professional Students
- Financial Aid for Freshmen Student
- Financial Aid for Minorities
- Financial Aid for Women
- Financial Aid for Disabled Students

Federal Programs

The U.S. Federal government provides over 75% of financial aid awarded to students attending a college, university, professional, technical, vocational, or accredited school in the United States. The federal government offers several grant, loan, and work-study programs to help students pay for their education. In order to receive financial assistance from the federal government, you must complete the Free Application for Federal Student Aid (FAFSA) (www.fafsa.ed.gov).

The Free Application for Federal Student Aid (FAFSA) is used by the U.S. Department of Education to determine your Expected Family Contribution (EFC) and eligibility for certain Student Financial Assistance (SFA) Programs. Many state education agencies and institutions also use the information submitted on your FAFSA to determine your eligibility for their State and Institutional Aid, respectively.

Student Financial Assistance (SFA) Programs (www.ed.gov/studentaid/) consist of:
- Federal Pell Grants
- Campus-Based Programs
- Federal Supplemental Opportunity Grants (FSEOG)
  - Federal Work-Study (FWS)
  - Federal Perkins Loans
- Federal Family Education Loan (FFEL) Program
  - Federal Stafford Loans (Subsidized and Unsubsidized)
  - Federal PLUS Loans
- William D. Ford Federal Direct Loan (Direct Loan) Program
  - Direct Loans (Subsidized and Unsubsidized)
  - Direct PLUS Loans

The Student Guide is the most comprehensive resource on student financial aid from the U.S. Department of Education. This guide will provide you with detailed information on: student eligibility, financial need, dependency status, applying, special circumstances, withdrawals, deadlines, types of Student Federal Aid (award amounts, interest, etc.), borrower responsibilities and rights, important terms, telephone numbers and web sites, and more. This publication is updated each award year. *The Student Guide* is available in English and Spanish, in which a copy can be downloaded from the U.S Department of Education's web site at www.studentaid.ed.gov/guide. You will need the Adobe Acrobat Reader (www.adobe.com) to view and print this document.

State Education Agencies

All states have one or more state education agencies that offer various financial aid programs to students. State education agencies award their financial aid on a first-come, first-serve basis. Typically, State Aid is restricted to their state's students attending a state school. You should contact your state's education agencies (**See Appendix** for a listing of State Education Agencies: State Department of Education) and request a financial aid guide detailing their State Aid and eligibility requirements. This information may be posted on their web site.

Provided below is a list of various State Aid programs:
- State Scholarship & Grant Programs
- Prepaid Tuition and College Savings Plans
- State Loan Program
- State Student Incentive Grant Program
- Loan-forgiveness programs for specific professions (i.e. education or health)
- State Employment Programs
- Financial Aid for Returning Adults
- Financial Aid for International Students
- Financial Aid for Graduate & Professional Students
- Financial Aid for Freshmen Student
- Financial Aid for Minorities
- Financial Aid for Women
- Financial Aid for Disabled Students

Private Loans (a.k.a. Alternative Loans)

Private loans are administered by private lenders to help supplement the government's Student Financial Assistance (SFA) programs, whenever students have borrowed the maximum loan amount from the SFA program. Private lenders offer different types of private loans to undergraduate and graduate students based on their level of study. Some private lenders also offer loans to relatives or friends that are willing to take out a loan on behalf of the student for educational purposes.

Private lenders often require a credit check and/or an income-to-debt ratio check on the borrower, co-signer, or both. They usually charge a higher interest rate than the government's student loan programs, but private lenders offer competitive interest rates, deferred payments, and flexible repayment options. You and/or your parent(s) must complete a loan application to apply for a private loan. There are no federal forms to complete to apply for a private loan.

Private loans are available from a variety of sources such as institutions, banks, credit unions, employers, and family members. Other loans such as home equity or personal loans are not specifically targeted for educational purposes, but may be used to pay for college costs.

Many parents seek private loans whenever they are seeking flexible repayment options such as deferring loan payments during their child's enrollment in school or until graduation. Deferring loan payments are not available under the Federal PLUS Loan program, in which repayment begins 60 days after the final loan disbursement for the academic year.

If you or your parents are considering a private loan, it is wise to compare interest rates and repayment options to those of other private lenders. Your school's financial aid office or state's education agency should have a list of private lenders.

There are several questions loan applicants should ask about any loan. These questions are only suggestions.
1. What is the interest rate?
2. Is the interest rate Fixed or Variable?
3. When does the loan have to be repaid?
4. What are the repayment terms and options?
5. How is the check disbursed?
6. What are the origination fees, guaranty fees, and any other additional or hidden fees?
7. What are the forbearance and deferment terms and conditions?

As borrower, you should:
- Read and understand the terms and conditions of each loan before you sign, anything. Eliminate any misunderstandings you may have about your loan.
- Know your Rights, Responsibilities, and the Consequences of defaulting on a loan.
- Always inform the lender, if you have an address change and/or changed schools.
- Whenever you speak with a loan representative, you should keep a log of the date, time, loan representative's name(s) of who you spoke too, and notes about the conversation.
- READ & SAVE EVERYTHING YOU SIGN!
  Save all promissory letters, check stubs, deferment / forbearance letter, disclosure statements, canceled checks, any and everything regarding the loan.

College Savings Plans

Congress passed Section 529 of the tax code, which allows two kinds of College Savings Plans for parents. These savings plans allow parents to save for their children's education depending on their needs and goals. Each plan has its advantages and disadvantages.

The two kinds of College Savings Plans are the:
- Prepaid Tuition Plans
- 529 College-Savings Plans

You can find detailed information about each plan at:

- **The College Savings Plans Network** (www.collegesavings.org)
  The official 529-plan web site, sponsored by the State Treasurer's Association, provides links to plans in your state.

- **Saving For College** (www.SavingForCollege.com)
  Operated by Joseph Hurley, this web site provides regular updates on College Savings Plans. You can find details about each plan's strengths and weaknesses.

Education Tax Benefits

In August of 1997, the Taxpayer Relief Act was signed into law. IRS Publication 970 "Tax Benefits for Higher Education" explains the various tax benefits and credits for individuals and family members continuing their education. You should consult a tax advisor or financial planner to discuss the advantages and disadvantages of each tax benefit for your family's situation, if needed. Download a copy of IRS Publication 970 (www.irs.gov) or call the IRS at 800-829-3676 (voice).

IRS Publication 970 explains in detail the following tax benefits and credits:
- Education Tax Credits
  - Hope Credit
  - Lifetime Learning Credit
- Education Individual Retirement Accounts (renamed the Coverdell Education Savings Accounts)
- Penalty-free withdrawals from Traditional or Roth IRAs
- Deduction for student loan interest
- Cancellation of certain student loans
- Qualified State Tuition Programs
- Interest earned on certain savings bonds
- Employer-provided Educational Assistance Benefits

Military Educational Benefits & Programs

There are various military educational benefits and programs offered to military personnel, spouses, their children, and veterans. Provided below is a list of programs for you to review:

- ROTC Scholarships
  ROTC scholarships are awarded to hundreds of students each year at college campuses across the United States. These scholarships are awarded strictly on merit – to the most outstanding students who apply, regardless of their family's financial status. ROTC scholarships vary based on the branch of service and the type and/or length of the scholarship. ROTC scholarships provide money for college tuition, educational fees, books, and in some cases a monthly allowance. Scholarship recipients participate in summer training during their enrollment in college and must fulfill their military obligation, either active duty or reserve service, after graduation. If you are interested in learning more about the various ROTC Programs, you should contact a ROTC representative at your school.

- Military Service Academies' Scholarships
  The U.S. Military Service Academies offer young men and women the opportunity to earn a college degree (Bachelor of Science Degree) and commission as an officer for the U.S. Armed Forces. The Army, Navy, Air Force, Merchant Marine, and Coast Guard have their own Service Academy. An education received from one of the academies is ranked among the best in the nation. Military Service Academies award full scholarships to students accepted for admission, which covers tuition, room and board. Each student also receives a monthly stipend to pay for books, supplies, clothing, and personal expenses. If you are interested in learning more about the Military Service Academies, you should contact a military service academy representative.

- U.S. Armed Forces Educational Benefits
  The U.S. Armed Forces offer a wide range of scholarships and educational programs to personnel, spouses, their children, and veterans. Each branch of the service offers the same basic military benefits. These programs change often and have specific eligibility requirements. Some branches may offer special incentives such as enlistment bonuses of extra college funds and service specific programs.

  By joining any branch of the military you may qualify for a wide range of educational benefits, but they all have the following common benefits:
  - Montgomery GI Bill:
    - Active Duty (MGIB-AD)
    - Selected Reserve (MGIB-SR)
  - Veterans Educational Assistance Program (VEAP)
  - Survivors' and Dependents' Educational Assistance Program (DEA)
  - Work-Study Program
  - Tuition Assistance

  The VA Education Service, which administers several Educational Benefits Programs, provides general and detailed information for each benefits program on their web site. Visit the Veteran Affair's web site at www.gibill.va.gov/ or call GI Bill at 1-888-GI-BILL-1 (1-888-442-4551) to speak with a Veterans Benefits Counselor for additional information.   The U.S. Armed Forces recruiting offices may also provide information about educational benefits offered by the military.

- Service Specific Programs
  There are other service specific programs available that offer educational benefits and programs. The Army offers a College First program and the Coast Guard has the CSPI program.

- Military Organizations
  Some military organizations offer scholarships to their members, members' spouse, and/or their children. Contact the organization's you and/or your parents are members to inquire about possible scholarships.

Libraries & Librarians

The local and main libraries in your city have various books, directories, and magazines on the subject of financial aid. These books are usually located in the reference section. It is important to review the most recent editions, since scholarship information changes each year. Some libraries have computers available for visitors to search their scholarship database or free scholarship search directories on the Internet. Ask the librarian, if he/she is aware of any scholarships offered by their library or organizations that donate books to their library.

SAT & ACT Exams

If you are a high school student, it will be in your best interest to take the Preliminary SAT (PSAT) or ACT (PACT) exam. The reasons for taking these practice exams are to possibly increase your test scores and prepare you for the actual exam. Most schools and some scholarship providers will require that you take one of these exams. The higher your SAT or ACT scores, you increase your chances of being admitted to the school(s) of your choice and receiving Merit-Based scholarships. Therefore, it would be in your best interest to study and take the practice exams to receive a high score, the first time you take the exam.

Visit the following web sites for additional information:
- College Board Online (www.collegeboard.org/)
- ETS Net The Educational Testing Service Network (www.ets.org/body.html)
- SAT Math Prep Site (www.gomath.com/sat1/index3.html)
- Kaplan SAT (www.kaplan.com/precoll/sat_top.html)
- Kaplan ACT (www.kaplan.com/precoll/act_top.html)
- Princeton Review SAT (www.review.com/college/sat/)
- ACT Home Page (www.act.org)
- Vocabulary.com (www.vocabulary.com/)

Internet – Free Scholarship Search Directories

There are numerous free scholarship search directories on the Internet. These online directories will help make your scholarship search process easy.

Here's how a typical online scholarship search directory works:

1. You will complete a scholarship questionnaire by answering several questions about your education, academic goals, career goals, extracurricular activities, ethnicity, religious affiliation, artistic talents, athletic talents, parent's background and affiliations, and other information.
2. The directory then matches your answers to the scholarships' eligibility requirements within its database.
3. After matching scholarships to your profile, it will provide you with a list of scholarships. When you click on each scholarship's name, you will be presented with a scholarship profile. A scholarship profile usually includes the sponsor's complete contact information, scholarship purpose and guidelines, eligibility requirements, award amount(s), deadline date, and supporting documents required to complete the application process. It is your responsibility to request an application from the scholarship provider by visiting their web site, emailing, writing, or calling.

To find several online scholarship search directories, you should type in the keywords "scholarship search" into any Internet search engine such as Google.com. The Internet search engine results will provide you with numerous web sites for you to choose from. From the results page, you should select a web site to start your free scholarship search.

Note: Avoid agencies, organizations, and web sites that offer to conduct a scholarship search for you for a fee and "Beware of Scholarship Scams." If you have a few hours a week and access to the Internet (or scholarship publications located at your local libraries or bookstores), you can obtain the same information for free.

Banks / Credit Unions

Many banking institutions and credit unions offer scholarships to students in their community, bank account holders, and/or their children. Contact the bank or credit union that you and your parent(s) have an active bank account and inquire about any scholarships offered by their banking institution. You should consult your *Yellow Pages* to obtain contact information of other banking institutions and credit unions in your community and city. Once you have the banks' telephone numbers, you should call and inquire about scholarships offered to students.

Employers

Some companies offer financial assistance to their employees and/or employees' children interested in furthering their education. The employer's human resource or benefits department should be able to inform your parents about the types of financial assistance offered by their company. Some employers may offer:

- Employer Tuition Programs
  Some employers offer tuition assistance programs for employees considering going back to school. According to IRS regulations, employers can provide up to $5,250 to each employee per year on a tax-free basis. Additional employer tuition assistance is taxed; so many employers stay within the IRS guidelines and limit. The IRS Publication 970 (www.irs.gov) can provide you with additional information about the employer-provided educational assistance benefits.

  If your employer is willing to invest in your future, it is important that you understand their polices and guidelines such as: GPA requirements, tuition payment / reimbursement programs, career/major requirements, post-degree work requirements, payment for books and materials, completion schedule for courses/degree, etc.

- Scholarships
  Some employers offer scholarships to employees and/or employees' children. Ask your parents to contact their employer's human resource or benefits department regarding scholarships for employees' children. If their employer offers scholarships for students, your parents should request an application.

  If you are working part-time for a company that offers scholarships to its employees, you should contact your supervisor, the human resource or benefits department to learn more about the scholarship's eligibility requirements. If you are eligible to apply, you should request an application.

- Employer Loans
  Some employers offer low interest-rate college loans to employees and/or employees' children.

Volunteer - Make A Difference

Volunteering your time is an excellent opportunity to become a well-rounded individual, improve your chances of winning a scholarship, and enlighten your life. Remember that most scholarship providers look for students who are involved in their community, outside activities, and have good grades. Some volunteer organizations also offer scholarships.

Public Officials

Your state's representatives, mayor, governor, or other public officials in your community and city may offer scholarships to students continuing their education. Public officials usually have an office that handles their normal business affairs. You should contact the officials in your state, city, and community. Their telephone numbers are listed in the *Yellow Pages* within the Government section. Ask the receptionist, if the public official (state the official's name, i.e. Mr. John Doe) offer scholarships for students or know of associates who sponsor students continuing their education. You should also visit the web site of your state, city, and county government, in which some scholarship information may be posted on their web site. Remember, the government is a networking community and there is always someone who knows someone. So Network!

Organizations, Associations, Unions

Various professional organizations, associations, and labor unions offer scholarships to members and their children. Many of these organizations offer scholarships that are not well publicized, which are usually small in amount (less than $1,000). You should consider contacting professional and social organizations that you and your parents are members.

You should also research organizations that represent your career field, and contact them to inquire about any scholarships offered to students. Some organizations require scholarship applicants to be members. If this is a requirement, you should join as a member (if interested).

Chamber of Commerce

The Chamber of Commerce is an association of member companies, civic and professional organizations, trade associations, and leaders in the business community. Each state and city has a Chamber of Commerce office. You should contact the Chamber of Commerce in your city and where you will attend school, and ask if they have a members and/or scholarship directory. Once you obtain a listing of its members, you should contact each business and organization to inquire about any scholarships offered to students furthering their education. Many local businesses and organizations offer small scholarships (less than $1,000) to students in their community. There are also Chamber of Commerce divisions for ethnic communities such as African Americans, Hispanics, etc. Many of their scholarships are not well publicized; you will be surprised that some scholarships are not awarded each year.

Visit your state's and city's Chamber of Commerce web sites and browse them for scholarship information. The US Chamber of Commerce (www.uschamber.org/Chambers/Chamber+Directory/) has an online directory for each state. Within each state, there is a listing of cities with links to local Chamber of Commerce offices. Remember, the Chamber of Commerce is a networking community and there is always someone who knows someone. So Network!

Conventions / Trade Shows / Conferences

Each year, there are several conventions, trade shows, and conferences sponsored by professional organizations and businesses in the industry you are interested in pursuing as a career. If there is an event in your city, it would be in your best interest to attend one or more of these events to start networking and inquiring about scholarship and internship opportunities. You should visit each booth and attend as many seminars as possible (if interested) at the events you attend. Some events will charge a fee to gain access to the exhibitors' booth area and other scheduled events. It is a good idea to obtain a copy of the event's program guide to contact a few companies and organizations listed at a later date. Trade magazines usually provide a calendar of events of the names and dates for various events in their industry.

Scholarship, College, and Industry Directories

There are numerous directories about scholarships and financial aid at the bookstore and library in your community.

- Scholarship Directories
  Scholarship directories are designed to help students identify various sources of scholarships and financial aid to help pay for their education. These directories profile various scholarships. A scholarship profile usually includes the scholarship sponsor's complete contact information, scholarship purpose and guidelines, eligibility requirements, award amount(s), deadline date, and supporting documents required to complete the application process. When reviewing the scholarship directories, make sure you review the most recent editions since scholarship guidelines, eligibility requirements, and deadlines often change. There are also scholarship directories specifically for minorities, women, sports/athletics, and students with disabilities.

- College Directories
  College directories profile various colleges, universities, community colleges, vocational, and technical schools. These directories contain complete contact information, programs offered, sports, extracurricular activities, and more. More importantly, some directories will list the types of financial aid offered by the schools to students.

- Industry Directories
  Each industry has an industry directory with a complete listing of corporations, companies, professional organizations, and industry groups. You can locate your industry's directory on the Internet or at your local library. Once you find your career field's industry directory, you should contact some of the companies and organizations, and inquire about any scholarships offered to students.

If you still have time to devote to your scholarship search, you should go to the library and consult Gale's Encyclopedia of Associations. It also lists the names and contact information of professional associations, industry groups, ethnic societies, religious groups, and advocacy groups for minorities and women. You should make a list of all the companies and organizations that have a connection to your career field, and call them to inquire about scholarship opportunities. Many of their scholarships are not well publicized; you will be surprised that some scholarships are not awarded each year.

Magazines

Magazines are great resources to review for scholarships, internships, and career opportunities. Many of these publications are often overlooked. Most popular and industry magazines provide helpful articles and information for its readers about scholarships and financial aid. These articles usually appear in the August, September, December, or January issues. You should review the various magazines that you and your parents read for scholarship information. Don't overlook magazines that represent your community, ethnic background, industry, sports, hobbies and interest, religious affiliation, military affiliation, etc. Some organizations and businesses specifically target the magazine's subscribers to help students continue their education.

There is a listing of the magazines' advertisers in the last few pages of the magazine. You should contact each advertiser and ask if they offer scholarships or would be interested in sponsoring a student whose pursuing a career within their industry.

Newspapers

Some scholarships are announced in your school, community, city, and national newspapers. These scholarships are usually announced in the Money, Education, and/or Career section of each newspaper.

Churches / Religious Organizations

Churches and religious organizations offer scholarships to its members and some offer them to students in their community. You should contact your church or a church in your community for additional scholarship information.

Internships / Cooperative (Co-Op) Education Programs

Internships and cooperative education programs allow students to apply their skills and knowledge learned in the classroom to actual on-the-job experiences. Many employers offer these programs for students to learn more about a particular career field, gain real world work experience, and possibly earn money to help pay for their education. Most schools have formed partnerships with various companies to employ their students. These programs are not based on financial need and are available to undergraduate, graduate, and professional students.

Searching for an internship or cooperative education program is very similar to conducting a scholarship or full-time job search. The key to a successful internship search is identifying all of your available resources. Ask your academic advisor or department administrator about these programs.

Other effective ways to find an internship or co-op program are by:
- Searching the Internet.
- Reading through directories.
- Viewing bulletin boards.
- Asking professors and faculty members.
- Contacting the employers yourself.
- And never forget friends and family employed in the industry you are pursuing as a career. They may have connections in your career field and may be able to provide you with contacts as well.

Financial Planners

Financial planners are experts in the field of financial planning. Financial planners can offer parents information and advice on the best ways to finance their child's college education through investments and money savings strategies. There are several types of financial planners (i.e. Certified Financial Planner (CFP), Chartered Financial Consultant (ChFC)) that offer different services. The services a financial planner offers may depend on various factors such as their credentials, licenses, and/or areas of expertise.

Unfortunately, financial planners charge a FEE for their services. Financial planners are paid for the services they provide through fees, commissions, or a combination of both. The fee a financial planner charges usually depends on his/her level of service, experience, and your needs. Before your parents decide to hire a financial planner, they should do their homework and learn more about the planner's qualifications, credentials, and reputation. Just remember, your parents should shop around for a financial planner as they would for a car or loan.

The following list of organizations can assist your parents with additional information on selecting a financial planner, locating one or more planners in their area, and checking the planner's qualifications and credentials. These organizations may offer a free referral program. Your parents should contact the following organizations to inquire about their services.

Financial Planning Association
Toll Free: 800.322.4237
Telephone: 404.845.0011
Fax: 404.845.3660
www.fpanet.org/

Certified Financial Planner Board of Standards
Telephone: 303-830-7500
Fax: 303-860-7388
www.CFP-Board.org/

American Society of CLU & ChFC
Telephone: 610-526-2500
Fax: 610-527-1499
www.financialpro.org/

American Institute of Certified Public Accountants
Telephone: 888-777-7077
Fax: 201-938-3750
www.aicpa.org/

WARNING!

Beware of Scholarship Scams

Families should avoid companies that charge a fee and make claims about guaranteeing scholarships and financial aid for school. The information these companies provide can be found free of charge on scholarship search directories on the Internet, bookstores, libraries, and in most colleges' financial aid office.

Keep in mind:
- No one can promise that you will receive financial aid.
- No one knows you better than you.
- Why pay someone to do the work for you, when it's your education and career - take control.

The Federal Trade Commission (FTC) launched Project Scholarship Scam (www.ftc.gov/bcp/conline/edcams/scholarship/) to alert families and consumers about potential scholarship scams and how to recognize them. Here are the FTC's six basic warning signs and advice:

1. "The scholarship is guaranteed or your money back."
    No one can guarantee that you will receive a scholarship. If you decide to use a company that charges a fee, you should request information about their refund policies in writing.

2. "You can't get this information anywhere else."
    Check with your school or library before you decide to pay someone to do the work for you. If you decide to use one of these services, you should check their reputation by contacting the Better Business Bureau (www.bbb.org) or your State's Attorney Office.

3. "May I have your credit card or bank account number to hold this scholarship?"
    Don't give out your credit card or bank account number over the phone without getting information in writing first. It may be a set-up for an unauthorized charge or withdrawal.

4. "We'll do all the work for you."
    Don't fall for this scam. They will ask you numerous questions, and then search their scholarship database or another company's database. So they need your help. There's no way around it. You should apply for each scholarship or grant, yourself.

5. The scholarship will cost some money.
    Do not pay anyone who claims to be "holding" a scholarship or grant for you.   Free money should not cost a thing.

6. "You've been selected by a national foundation to receive a scholarship." or "You're a finalist." in a contest you never entered. Before you send money to apply for a scholarship, you should do some research on the company. Make sure the foundation or program is legitimate.

The Federal Trade Commission (FTC) works for the consumer to prevent fraudulent, deceptive, and unfair business practices in the marketplace. The FTC also provides information to help consumers spot, stop and avoid fraud. To file a complaint or to get free information on consumer issues, visit the FTC web site at www.ftc.gov/ftc/consumer.htm or call toll-free 1-877-FTC-HELP (1-877-382-4357).

What's Next?

By now, you should have identified several sources that offer scholarships and financial aid that you want to contact and request an application. As you prepare to start your scholarship search, use your time wisely to apply to as many scholarships that you are eligible to receive. It is important to read the eligibility requirements for each scholarship. If you do not meet the scholarship's eligibility requirements, DO NOT request an application or apply for the award. Don't waste your time or the scholarship provider's time. Your next step is Chapter 4: Completing the Scholarship Application.

Chapter 4
Completing the Scholarship Application

Chapter 4 will help you complete the scholarship application process. The entire scholarship application process can be time-consuming. There are numerous steps and supporting documents you must gather and submit to the scholarship provider. If you start your scholarship search early and stay organized, you will complete your scholarship application(s) in a timely fashion and keep your stress level to a minimum; and you will be glad that you did.

The following steps will help you complete the scholarship application process:
- Obtaining an Application
- Keeping Track of the Application
- Application Components
- Supporting Documents
- Completing the Application
- Completing an Online Application
- Creating a Competitive Application
- Putting the Application Package Together
- Submitting Your Application - On-time
- The Waiting Game
- Scholarship Interview
- Preparing for the Interview
- Interviewing Do's and Don'ts
- After the Interview
- After Winning a Scholarship
- Scholarship Disbursement
- Renewing Your Scholarship

Obtaining an Application

There are three methods in which you can obtain a scholarship application and learn more about the organization providing the scholarship, scholarship eligibility requirements, and past scholarship winners. Your options are:

- **Visiting the Scholarship Provider's Web Site**

  Most scholarship providers post information about their scholarship(s) on their web site. Posting scholarship information on their web site saves everyone time and money, which can make the difference in submitting your application before the deadline date. There are various types of scholarship applications on the Internet. The most common applications are: electronic (online) application and downloadable Portable Document Format (PDF). However, there are other types of applications such as MS Word Document and plain text applications.

  Before you start downloading and printing an application from the scholarship provider's web site, you should make sure the information and application is current.   If the web site specifies an application deadline for the previous year, the application and/or eligibility requirements may have changed. If you encounter this problem, you should request a print application directly from the scholarship provider by writing, emailing, or calling.

- **Writing or Emailing**

  Writing or emailing the scholarship provider is another method used to request and obtain an application. If you use this method, you must create a request letter. Your request letter should be brief and to the point. It should briefly describe your educational and career goals, and request an application. You should type your request letter and make sure that it is neat and free of spelling and grammatical errors. You can use the same letter to request an application from other scholarship providers, but make sure you change the scholarship provider's name and the date.

  Some scholarship providers offer multiple scholarship awards. If you encounter a scholarship provider offering multiple scholarships, you should specify the name of the scholarship for which you are requesting an application in your request letter. If you are requesting multiple scholarship applications offered by the same scholarship provider, you can list all the scholarship names in your request letter. **Sample request letters** are located in the Appendix.

  If you have not received a response or application after 2 to 3 weeks, you should send another request letter. It is acceptable to use the original letter, but you must change the date. As a reminder, many scholarship providers are large organizations that receive many scholarship application requests; there is a chance that your first request letter was lost in the "paper shuffle." If you sent a second request letter and still have not received an application, the sponsoring organization may no longer offer the scholarship. If there is a telephone number available, you should call the organization to inquire about the existence of the scholarship. Use common sense when speaking with a scholarship provider - Don't be RUDE!

- **Calling**

  If you are going to call the scholarship provider, remember to be polite to the receptionist. If a scholarship provider's telephone, fax, or email address is not included with their contact information, this is a clear indication that they do not want applicants to contact them by that method. If you encounter this problem, visit their web site or write a request letter.

Keeping Track of Applications

Once you start receiving the scholarship applications and gathering supporting documents, you should create a separate file folder for each scholarship. Write the name of each scholarship and deadline date on the tab or front of the folder. Everything that you receive and gather (i.e. brochures, recommendation letter, resume, application, etc.) for each scholarship should be placed in its folder. File folders will also keep everything clean and neat, especially the scholarship application.

To help you remember important dates and stay on track, you should buy a calendar and mark the deadline date for each scholarship application and other important date(s), and place it where you will constantly see it.

Application Components

Before you start filling out the scholarship application, lets review the most common components of any scholarship application. All scholarship applications have different instructions and request varying information. However, scholarship applications request the same basic information from each applicant.

There are five – six components of most scholarship applications:
1. Contact Information
2. College and Career Plans
3. Education
4. Extracurricular Activities
5. Achievements, Awards, Honors
6. Supporting Documents

Supporting Documents

Most scholarship providers request supporting documents to accompany your completed scholarship application. Supporting documents give the scholarship committee a "3 Dimensional Picture" of you. These documents can tell the scholarship committee more about you than your answers on the application. In many cases, supporting documents have been the deciding factor as to who will win the scholarship. This is your opportunity to sell yourself and show the committee that you are the most deserving candidate for their scholarship.

There are various types of supporting documents such as:

- **Academic Transcript**
  An academic transcript is an official record of all your grades from high school or college. It is not the same as your report card. If you attended more than one school, you will need to request a transcript from each school. In order to save yourself some time, you should order several transcripts from your school and place them in a clean envelope or folder. Some colleges charge their students a fee to fulfill their request for a transcript.

  It is important that you follow the application's instructions on how to submit your transcript. Some scholarship providers prefer to have the transcript mailed directly to them, while others like to have it included with the completed scholarship application package. If you are instructed to have your school mail the transcript directly to the scholarship provider, it is also important to provide your school with the correct mailing address to ensure that the scholarship provider receives your transcript. It would be in your best interest to contact your school to make sure they mailed your transcripts. If you are instructed to include your transcript with your application, do not open or tamper with the transcript's sealed envelope. If the sealed envelope is opened, the scholarship provider may reject your application.

- **Official SAT or ACT test score(s)**
  If you are a high school student, you may have to submit an official copy of your most recent SAT or ACT test score(s) with most of your scholarship applications. A copy of your official SAT or ACT test score(s) must be requested from the testing organization. The test registration booklet and your score report should tell you how to request additional test scores.

  You can request additional score reports online:
  - ACT Score (www.act.org/aap/scores/online2.html)
  - SAT Score (www.collegeboard.com/student/testing/sat/scores.html)

  When you request additional score reports, you will have to pay a fee and provide the scholarship provider's code to which the score report is being sent too. The online score report request form has a listing of codes for colleges and scholarship providers for you to choose from. If you do not find your scholarship provider's code on the score report form, you should contact the scholarship provider to request their scholarship code. After completing the request form, your test scores will be sent to the scholarship provider(s).

- **Essay / Personal Statement**
  Most scholarship providers will request applicants to write an essay or personal statement. The essay/personal statement is one of the most important parts of any scholarship application. Without an essay/personal statement, every application will look the same with the same basic information (i.e. grades, financial need, extracurricular activities, etc.). The essay is a key factor in deciding whether an applicant is invited to an interview or awarded the scholarship.

  The essay/personal statement is a self-portrait of you. It offers an insightful view of yourself (i.e. values, experiences, dream, etc.), your method of thinking, ability to communicate, and write effectively. Your essay/personal statement will provide an added dimension to the application, which can "make" or "break" your application.

  Scholarship essay/personal statements often cover the same topics as college application essays. You may be able to reuse or revise previous essays written for other college and scholarship applications to use for new scholarship essays. This does not mean that you should write one very general essay/personal statement to use for every scholarship application. If you reuse an essay that you previously wrote, you must revise it and tailor it to each individual scholarship. You may have to write a new essay to address the essay question on a scholarship application. If you kept copies of all previously written essays, you may have saved yourself a lot of time.

  Note: Once applicants realize that an essay/personal statement is required, most applicants never submit their applications - thus eliminating themselves out of the competition. Here's something to think about: If you spend 10 hours writing an essay (from beginning to end) for a $1000 scholarship and you win it -- that is $100 per hour and at your age, this will be the best hourly wage ever!

- **Resume**
  A scholarship resume is your SALES TOOL. It is slightly different than a job resume. The major focus of a scholarship resume is your education, extracurricular activities, achievements, awards and honors. A job resume basically focuses on your work experiences and skills. Do not use a job resume when applying for a scholarship. Refer to **Chapter 2: The Workbook – Part VII: Resume Template** for more details about creating a scholarship resume.

- **Letter of Recommendation**
  Most scholarship providers will request two or three letters of recommendation from individuals that you know such as a reference. Letters of recommendation allow the scholarship committee to form an idea of who you are as an individual through someone else's opinion. These letters can be extremely important, and they should reveal information about you that is not necessarily mentioned in your application, resume, test scores, etc. A good letter of recommendation can often be persuasive to the scholarship committee, especially if there is a "borderline" decision between you and another applicant. Refer to **Chapter 2: The Workbook – Part VI: References** for more details about - Who to ask to write a letter of recommendation.

- **References**
  Some scholarship providers may request a list of references. Your references should be listed on a sheet of paper with their names and complete contact information (i.e. address, telephone, email address, etc.), as well as your relationship to those references. References are used to gain an idea of what others think about you. Select your references carefully. A good reference is someone who knows you well. He/she should be able to answer questions about your character, academics, leadership, teamwork, and/or extracurricular activities. Refer to **Chapter 2: The Workbook – Part VI: References** for more details about - Who to ask to be references.

- **Samples of Artwork or Performances**
  Scholarship providers that award scholarships based on students' artistic or athletic talents will most likely want to see samples of their artwork or performances. If you have to submit copies of your artwork, performances, or writing samples, the most important thing to remember is to follow the application's instructions on how to submit these materials.

  For example: If the scholarship application requests a 5-minute cassette tape and you send a 10-minute CD, your application may be disqualified, because you did not follow the instructions. If you have any questions about how to prepare your materials, you should contact the scholarship provider regarding your questions.

- **Auditions**
  If you are applying for a performing arts scholarship for music, drama, theater, dance, etc., the scholarship provider may require an audition to assess your skills. It is important that you understand and adhere to the audition's requirements.

- **Photograph**
  Some scholarship applications may request a photograph to be used for publicity purposes after winners are chosen. A recent color or black and white photograph, no larger than four by six (4x6) inches, should accompany your application package (if requested). Do not enclose candid snapshots or baby pictures. It would be a wise decision to send a photograph of you in a suit or casual attire.

- **Federal Income Tax Information**
  Some organizations that award scholarships based on financial need may request a copy of you and/or your parents Federal Income Tax Return Form 1040. The federal income tax forms are used to verify your family's income.

- **Copy of Certificate(s), Rating(s), or License(s)**
  Some scholarship providers may request copies of your certificates, ratings, or licenses. You should make several copies of these documents to save yourself time and place them in an envelope or folder.

In order to save time, you should also begin preparing and gathering some of these documents before the application arrives. Once, you have this information, it is wise to keep all of your documents in an oversized envelope or folder to keep them clean and neat.   Remember - first impressions are a lasting impression. So be CLEAN and NEAT! The importance of planning ahead cannot be overstressed.

Completing the Application

Once you receive the scholarship application, it is very important to read and follow all instructions. If you have any questions, do not hesitate to call the scholarship provider. Failure to follow instructions and/or submit the supporting documents may disqualify your application. Remember, each scholarship has its own set of rules and deadline date, so follow the instructions carefully.

After you have read all the instructions, you should make several copies of the original application to use as drafts. Place the original application in its scholarship folder to keep it neat and clean. If you completed **Chapter 2: The Workbook**, you should refer to each part to help you complete the draft application. It may take you several drafts to complete a final draft application, until it is accurate and free of spelling and grammatical errors. When your final draft application is complete, you must transfer your information correctly to the original scholarship application.

Completing an Online Application

An online scholarship application can be completed and submitted over the Internet via the scholarship provider's web site. Before you complete the online application, you should print a copy of the online application to use as a draft application. After printing the application, you should bookmark the scholarship provider's web site, so you can easily return to the online application when you are ready to complete and submit the application.

Once you have completed your final draft application with no spelling or grammatical errors, you should return to the scholarship provider's web site, refer to your final draft application, and carefully type your answers into each blank provided on the online scholarship application. After you have completed the online application, you should review your answers to ensure that your application is free of any mistakes or errors (i.e. grammatical, punctuation, and spelling errors), print a copy for your records, and then click the 'Submit' button to submit your application.   You may be required to mail any supporting documents requested by the scholarship provider.

Creating a Competitive Application

A competitive application is neat, clean, and complete. In order to give yourself a competitive edge, you should type the original application. Typing your application ensures that it will be legible, uniform, and professional in appearance. Before you type on the original application, you should make draft copies and practice on them to figure out how much space you have for each answer and where to set the margins. When you are ready to transfer your information to the original scholarship application, take your time. Avoid mistakes by typing slowly to avoid using correction fluid.

If you do not have a typewriter, your local library should have a few typewriters for public access. You should also ask one of your school's teachers or counselors, if you could use their typewriter to type your scholarship application. If you do not have access to a typewriter, use your best hand writing skills and a black pin, and print legible.

Before you start completing the original application, you should make sure the surface where you are going to complete the application is clean by wiping it off with a clean wet cloth and then dry it off.

Once your application is complete, you should:
- Make sure it is free from stray marks, stains, and wrinkles.
- Proofread it to make sure it is free from spelling and grammatical errors.
- Have someone proofread your application.
- Make a copy of the completed application for your records.

Putting your Application Package Together

Scholarship providers will be impressed with the presentation and appearance of your scholarship application package. Once you have completed the application and gathered all the requested supporting documents, it is important to present the entire package in a professional manner and submit it on time.

Advice
- Do not staple or paperclip materials, unless the application directs you to do so.
- Unless told otherwise, you should arrange the supporting documents in the order outlined in the application's instructions.
- Type or print your name in the top corner of every page (be consistent in the location of your name) in case the application and supporting documents become separated.
- Use a large envelope to keep everything neat and wrinkle-free, and take it to the post office yourself to ensure that you attach the correct postage.

You should enclose a self-addressed, stamped envelope (SASE) with your application package. A SASE is an envelope addressed to you with the scholarship provider's name in the return address area of the envelope. Do not forget to add a stamp to your SASE.

Once the scholarship provider receives your application package with a SASE enclosed, they will mail the SASE back to you. When you receive your SASE, it will be an indication that the scholarship provider received your application package; and you should put the SASE in the folder along with the other information for that scholarship.

Your scholarship application package should:
- Convey that you are serious, professional, and a worthy applicant.
- Demonstrate that you are the most qualified applicant.
- Convey that you have the ability and desire to succeed in your chosen career.
- Make the scholarship provider want to offer you the scholarship.

Submitting Your Completed Application Package - On Time

Many scholarship applications are disqualified, because some applicants fail to submit their applications on-time. If an application's deadline date has passed, you should keep the information and apply next year.

There are 4 methods in which you can submit your completed scholarship package:

- **Online**

  An online application can be completed and submitted on the Internet through the scholarship provider's web site. When you are ready to complete and submit your application, you should return to the scholarship provider's web site, refer to your final draft application, and carefully type your answers into each blank provided on the online application. After completing your application, you should review your answers for any mistakes or errors (i.e. grammatical, punctuation, and spelling errors), print a copy of the online application for your records, and then click the 'Submit' button to submit your application. You may be required to mail any supporting documents requested by the scholarship provider.

- **Mail**

  Most scholarship providers indicate that your application must be postmarked or received at their office by a certain deadline date. If you are going to mail your application package, you have a few options to choose from such as:

  - First Class Mail

    If you mail your application package via First Class Mail, it will be in your best interest to mail the application package at least 5 - 7 business days (Saturday and Sunday are not considered business days) before the deadline date. The US Postal Office offers several methods to confirm that your application has been delivered: Registered Mail, Return Receipt Requested, and Certified Mail. Remember, a self-addressed, stamped envelope (SASE) will also confirm delivery of your application package. You should type your mailing labels to avoid any delivery delays.

  - Priority Mail

    Priority Mail is another service offered by the US Postal Office. The estimated delivery time is 2 - 3 days for delivery. Priority Mail is not a guaranteed service. If you decide to use Priority Mail, you should expect it to take four delivery days to be on the safe side.

  - Express Mail

    There are a few express carries that guaranteed next day and 2nd day delivery of your package.

- **Hand Deliver**
  If the scholarship provider's office is located in your city and you would like to hand deliver your application package, you should contact the organization to ensure this is an approved method. If you use this method, make sure you give your application package to the right individual or department, and take note of the person's name to whom you gave your application package.

- **Fax**
  It is rare, but some scholarship providers may accept faxed applications. Before you fax your application package, you should contact the organization to inform them that you are going to fax your scholarship application within a few minutes. After faxing your scholarship application package, you should print a confirmation report for your records, and then follow-up with a call to make sure that it was received in its entirety.

The Waiting Game

After submitting your scholarship application package, be patient and wait for an announcement of the winners. If you are not awarded the scholarship this year, you should reapply next year (if you meet the eligibility requirements).

Scholarship Interview

It is very unlikely that you will have to attend a scholarship interview, unless you are applying for a very prestigious scholarship. If you are invited to an interview, it is important that you prepare for the interview, as if it was for a job. This is your opportunity to meet the scholarship committee face-to-face and **SALE YOURSELF**.

Some interview questions are based on information provided in your scholarship application and supporting documents. Before the interview, you should review your scholarship application package and be prepared to discuss your educational background, work experiences, academic achievements, extracurricular activities, future plans, financial needs, and personal values. Researching information about the scholarship provider and past winners will help you prepare for any questions asked during the interview. During the interview, the scholarship committee will observe your overall appearance, attitude, personality, and how you communicate. They want to hear you speak about your abilities, career objectives, strengths, weaknesses, and more.

Provided below is a list of sample interview questions. Relate your actual experiences by including them into your answer(s). Don't falsify or memorize your answers to these question; you do not want to sound as if you are reading from a script. You also don't want to be caught off guard without an answer to basic questions.

Sample Interview Questions:
- Tell us about yourself?
- What would you like to achieve in college?
- What do you see yourself doing after college?
- Why should we award you this scholarship?
- What are your favorite academic subjects? Why?
- Give some examples of how you have demonstrated leadership skills?

- How are you involved in your community?
- What career field do you plan to pursue in college? Why?
- Why should we select you over the other applicants?
- Where do you see yourself five and/or ten years from now?
- What are your short and long-term goals?
- What are your strengths and weaknesses?

More specific questions may be asked depending on the type of organization and the scholarship. If the scholarship is designated for a particular ethnic group, club affiliation, etc., you should expect to answer a few questions relating to that area.

Ask Questions

The interviewer(s) will expect you to ask at least one question. Below are sample questions you may want to ask:

- What are the scholarship recipient's responsibilities?
- What is the selection process?
- When should I expect a response?
- Is the scholarship renewable?
- What are the renewal policies?
- Will I lose the scholarship, if I accept an internship, study abroad, or attend to personal/family matters?
- Will I lose the scholarship, if I change majors?
- Is there a probation period for poor academic progress or low grade point average?

Preparing for the Interview

Preparing for an interview may be a difficult task for some students. The easiest way to prepare for an interview is to have one or two 'mock' interviews. A mock interview consists of having someone (i.e. teacher, counselor, parent) pretend to be the interviewer and ask you several interview questions.

The mock interviewer should be able to critique your answers, appearance, presentation, etc. This feedback will help identify your strengths and weaknesses. You should ask the mock interviewer a few questions about your answers, what can you do better, how do you look and sound, etc. You do not want to appear unorganized or unprepared during the interview. You should be able to provide a confident answer to each question asked by the interviewer or scholarship committee.

The day before the interview, you should review information about the scholarship provider, the scholarship's purpose and guidelines, and your entire scholarship application package and supporting documents that you submitted to that scholarship provider. It is important that you remember what you submitted to the scholarship provider. You may not need it, but you should take a copy of your scholarship application package to the interview for your records.

Interviewing Do's & Don'ts
Here is a list of interviewing Do's and Don'ts:

Do's
- Be yourself.
- Answer each question honestly and truthfully.
- Answer questions as clearly as possible, and take your time to think over your answers.
- Try to incorporate your goals, qualities, and experiences into your answers.
- Use a firm handshake. Avoid using a crushing or weak handshake. While shaking the interviewer's hand, you should make eye contact.
- Make eye contact throughout the interview. You should focus your eyes on the interviewer, but don't stare. Maintaining good eye contact shows that you are attentive, confident, and respectful.
- Sit facing the interviewer. You want to project that you are alert and attentive. Positioning your body away from the interviewer may give the interviewer the impression that you are rude or not interested.
- Maintain good posture, but try to be relaxed. Avoid crossing your arms; this will make you seem defensive. You want to have an "open" appearance and seem interested at all times.
- Smile and laugh when appropriate.
- Show interest in the interviewer's background and organization.
- Bring a portfolio of your work, list of activities, newspaper clippings, etc. Only bring items that will contribute to your application and the interview.

Don'ts
- Do not try to be someone you are not.
- Do not dress casually. Do not show up in jeans, T-shirt, earrings, fancy jewelry, pagers, etc. Men should wear a conservative suit and tie. Women should wear a conservative dress or a pants suit, and avoid using excessive makeup.
- Do not arrive late. It is recommended that you arrive ten minutes early. This will give you time to relax. Arriving late does not give a good impression of you.
- Do not rush into answering the questions.
- Do not tell the interviewer what you think he/she wants to hear.
- Do not talk too much about one particular subject. Answer the question and move on. Do not go into details unless asked by the interviewer.
- Do not make inappropriate or rude comments. Avoid all of the following: profanity, jokes, personal comments about the interviewer, and political or religious comments. Things of this nature may eliminate you from the list of eligible applicants.
- Avoid nervous habits such as biting your nails, twiddling your thumbs, playing with a pen or pencil, shaking your leg, tapping your foot during the interview, etc. These habits and others may be distracting.
- Avoid drifting off while the interviewer is speaking. Pay attention and listen to what the interviewer is saying. Do not look out the window, at the furniture, or at the walls. Stay focused!
- Do not interrupt the interviewer when he/she is speaking.
- Words to avoid: "um," "like," or "you know", etc. In order to avoid these phrases, you should take a few moments before you respond and think about what you are going to say. Always try to provide a clear answer.
- Do not forget to thank the interviewer for his/her time and consideration.

After the Interview

After the interview, you should send the interviewer a 'Thank You' letter. A Thank You letter is an effective way of showing your gratitude. It should be short, simple, and sincere. You can add a personal touch by hand-writing the letter.

After Winning a Scholarship

After winning the scholarship, your job is not over. Scholarship providers expect you to continue to keep up the good work. If you start "slacking-off", you may jeopardize your scholarship and possibly your enrollment in school.

As a scholarship recipient, you should:

- Send a Thank You Letter
  Send a Thank You letter to show your gratitude and appreciation. It should be short, simple, and sincere. You can add a personal touch by handwriting the letter.

- Avoid "Senioritis"
  "Senioritis" (a.k.a. Senior Slump or Senior Slack) occurs when students start coasting through their senior year of high school, apparently spending more time working and partying and less time studying and completing "homework assignments." Your entire senior year is critical. However, the last semester of your senior year will be reviewed by the college you have chosen to attend, and the organization(s) that awarded you their scholarship(s). A poor performance (i.e. drop in grades) in the last semester of your senior year can result in your admittance to college and/or scholarship(s) being rescinded. You have worked too hard to see your efforts go down the "drain" by foolish mistakes in the last semester of school.

- Notify Your School's Financial Aid Office
  It is up to you to decide whether or not to inform your school's financial aid office about outside scholarship award(s) not listed on your financial aid package (i.e. award letter). If you do not notify your school, they may eventually find out about your outside scholarship award(s). Usually, this occurs whenever the scholarship provider submits the scholarship check directly to your school. If this is the case, the financial aid office will make adjustments as necessary. Avoid unpleasant surprises of receiving reduced financial aid or owing money back to the government or school. If you are unsure about how your outside scholarship award(s) will affect your financial aid package, you should contact your school's financial aid office to discuss your situation.

- Continue Your Scholarship Search
  Your goal should be to attend school for FREE. You should apply to as many scholarships in which you are eligible. If you find a winning strategy, you should stick to it.

Scholarship Disbursement

The scholarship provider should provide you with information on how the scholarship check will be disbursed, either directly to you or to the school. Most scholarship providers often require verification of enrollment or a billing statement from your school before disbursing the scholarship check. If this is the case, you must contact the Registrar's or Bursar's Office of your school to request that the appropriate documentation be mailed to the scholarship provider, or you can make a copy of your billing or registration statement and send (mail or fax) the information to the scholarship provider, yourself.

If you really need to know when you or the school will receive the scholarship check to prevent any enrollment problems such as class cancellations, you should contact the scholarship provider and ask when they intend to mail the scholarship check to avoid any problems. Once you receive this information, you should inform the Bursar's Office at your school. The Bursar's Office may grant you a payment extension.

Renewing Your Scholarship

If you receive a renewable scholarship, you must follow the scholarship provider's guidelines and policies in order to remain eligible for their scholarship. If you fail to maintain the organization's scholarship renewal requirements, you risk losing your scholarship. However, if you encounter unusual circumstances (such as personal/family hardship, serious illness, death of a family member, transfer to another school, change in career field – major, etc.), you should contact the scholarship provider(s) to discuss your circumstances. When you speak to someone about your circumstances regarding your scholarship, you should take notes of everyone you spoke to about your situation (i.e. name, date, time) and write a brief statement about the conversation for your records.

General renewal requirements may include, not limited to:
* Maintaining a minimum Grade Point Average (GPA).
* Enrollment Status (i.e. Full-time vs. Part-time enrollment status).
* Study within a designated career field.
* Enrollment at a particular school.
* Submitting copies of your current transcript or semester progress reports.

Appendix

- Sample Request Letters
- State Education Agencies (State Education Department)

(Date)

(Your Name)
(Address)
(City, State, Zip Code)
(Telephone Number)
(Email Address)

(Contact Person Name, if possible)
(Organization Name)
(Address)
(City, State, Zip Code)
(Telephone Number)
(Email Address)

Dear Scholarship Director (or Contact's Name),

My name is (place your name here) and (select one - I plan to or I am)- majoring in (indicate your field of study).

I am interested in receiving more information and an application for (Scholarship name).

Enclosed is a self-addressed, stamped envelope for your convenience in replying. Thank you for your time and consideration.

Sincerely,

(Your Signature)

(Your Name - Typed)

(Date)

(Your name)
(Address)
(City, State, Zip/Postal Code)
(Telephone Number)
(Email Address)

(Contact Person Name, if possible)
(Organization Name)
(Address)
(City, State, Zip Code)
(Telephone Number)
(Email Address)

Dear Scholarship Director (or Contact's Name),

My name is (place your name here) and (select one - I plan to or I am)- majoring in (indicate your field of study).

I am interested in receiving more information and an application for the following scholarships offered by your organization:
• (Scholarship name)
• (Scholarship name)
• (Scholarship name)
• (Scholarship name)

Enclosed is a self-addressed, stamped envelope for your convenience in replying. Thank you for your time and consideration.

Sincerely,

(Your Signature)

(Your Name - Typed)

State Education Agencies (State Department of Education)

This information is provided for your convenience. AvScholars Publishing, LLC. does not control or guarantee the accuracy, relevance, timeliness, or completeness of this outside information. Further, AvScholars Publishing, LLC. does not endorse any views expressed, or products or services offered by the organizations sponsoring these web sites.

State	Telephone	Web site URL
Alabama	(334) 242-9700	www.alsde.edu
Alaska	(907) 465-2800	www.eed.state.ak.us
Arizona	(602) 542-4361	www.ade.state.az.us
Arkansas	(501) 682-4204	arkedu.state.ar.us
California	(916) 319-0800	www.cde.ca.gov
Colorado	(303) 866-6600	www.cde.state.co.us
Connecticut	(860) 713-6548	www.state.ct.us/sde
Delaware	(302) 739-4601	www.doe.state.de.us
District of Columbia	(202) 724-4222	www.k12.dc.us
Florida	(850) 245-0505	www.fldoe.org
Georgia	(404) 656-2800	www.doe.k12.ga.us
Hawaii	(808) 586-3310	www.doe.k12.hi.us
Idaho	(208) 332-6800	www.sde.state.id.us/dept
Illinois	(217) 782-4321	www.isbe.state.il.us
Indiana	(317) 232-6610	www.doe.state.in.us
Iowa	(515) 281-3436	www.state.ia.us/educate
Kansas	(785) 296-3201	www.ksbe.state.ks.us
Kentucky	(502) 564-3421	www.kde.state.ky.us
Louisiana	(225) 342-4411	www.doe.state.la.us
Maine	(207) 624-6600	www.state.me.us/education/
Maryland	(410) 767-0100	www.msde.state.md.us
Massachusetts	(781) 338-3000	www.doe.mass.edu
Michigan	(517) 373-3324	www.michigan.gov/mde
Minnesota	(651) 582-8200	www.education.state.mn.us
Mississippi	(601) 359-3513	www.mde.k12.ms.us
Missouri	(573) 751-4212	www.dese.state.mo.us
Montana	(406) 444-2082	www.opi.state.mt.us
Nebraska	(402) 471-2295	www.nde.state.ne.us
Nevada	(775) 687-9141	www.nde.state.nv.us
New Hampshire	(603) 271-3495	www.state.nh.us/doe
New Jersey	(609) 292-4469	www.state.nj.us/education
New Mexico	(505) 827-5800	www.sde.state.nm.us
New York	(518) 474-5844	www.nysed.gov
North Carolina	(919) 807-3300	www.dpi.state.nc.us
North Dakota	(701) 328-2260	www.dpi.state.nd.us
Ohio	(614) 728-6698	www.ode.state.oh.us
Oklahoma	(405) 521-3301	www.sde.state.ok.us
Oregon	(503) 378-3600	www.ode.state.or.us
Pennsylvania	(717) 787-5820	www.pde.state.pa.us

State	Telephone	Web site URL
Rhode Island	(401) 222-4600	www.ridoe.net
South Carolina	(803) 734-8492	www.sde.state.sc.us
South Dakota	(605) 773-3553	www.state.sd.us/deca
Tennessee	(615) 741-2731	www.state.tn.us/education
Texas	(512) 463-9734	www.tea.state.tx.us
Utah	(801) 538-7500	www.usoe.k12.ut.us
Vermont	(802) 828-3135	www.state.vt.us/educ
Virginia	(804) 225-2023	www.pen.k12.va.us
Washington	(360) 725-6000	www.k12.wa.us
West Virginia	(304) 558-0304	wvde.state.wv.us
Wisconsin	(608) 266-3390	www.dpi.state.wi.us
Wyoming	(307) 777-7675	www.k12.wy.us
Department of Defense Schools		www.odedodea.edu
Bureau of Indian Affairs		www.oiep.bia.edu
American Somoa	(684) 633-5237	www.samoanet.com/asg/asgdoe97.html
Guam		www.doe.edu.gu
Northern Marianas	(670) 664-3721	www.pss.cnmi.mp
Puerto Rico	(787) 759-2000	www.eduportal.de.gobierno.pr/EDUPortal/default.htm
Virgin Islands	(340) 774-2810	www.networkvi.com/education

Customer Review

Tell us what you think. Write a review of The Scholarship Workbook™ and share your opinions with us and others. Your review should focus on the book's content and context. The best reviews include not only whether you liked or disliked a book, but also why.

Name: _____ **Title:** _____

School: _____

Location: _____

How do you rate The Scholarship Workbook™?

❑ 5 = Excellent ❑ 4 ❑ 3 ❑ 2 ❑ 1 = Poor

Share your review with us.

We want to know what you think about The Scholarship Workbook. Your comments will help us improve the workbook, and it will be shared with others. We will display your Real Name, title, and location (if you have provided us with this information) with your review on our web site.

_____
_____
_____
_____
_____
_____
_____
_____

How to submit your customer review.

You can submit your review:

Online: www.scholarship-workbook.com/review_form.htm

Fax: (801) 516-0639

Mail: AvScholars Publishing, LLC.
47 N. Cedar Lane
Glenwood, IL 60425

Thank you for submitting your customer review.

AvScholars Publishing, LLC. ▪ 47 N. Cedar Lane ▪ Glenwood, IL 60425
Tel: (773) 837-5931 ▪ Fax (801) 516-0639 ▪ Email: info@avscholars.com

The Scholarship Workbook Order Form

Complete this order form to purchase your Scholarship Workbook. Required fields are marked with an asterisk (*). **Type or Print legible.**

Shipping Information:

Name:* _____

Address:* _____

City:* _____ State/Province:* _____ Zip/Postal Code:* _____

Tel.:* _____ Email: _____

Product	Quantity	Price	Line Total
Scholarship Workbook		$16.95 each	
		Subtotal	$
		IL Sales Tax 7.75% - **See Note***	$
		Shipping & Handling – **See Note****	$
		Total	$

Sales Tax*

Illinois Sales Tax (7.75%) must be collected on Subtotal to shipments with an Illinois address.

Shipping and Handling**

- All orders are shipped US Postal Service –
  - o Priority Mail: $4.95
  - o Express Mail: $15.95
- Add $2 for each additional book ordered

Method of Payment

☐ **Check or Money Order Enclosed**
MAKE CHECK PAYABLE AND MAIL TO:
AvScholars Publishing, LLC.
47 N. Cedar Lane
Glenwood, IL 60425
P: (773) 837-5931 F: (801) 516-0639

☐ **Purchase Order**
Purchase orders accepted from educational institutions and government agencies only. COPY OF PURCHASE ORDER REQUIRED WITH THIS ORDER FORM

Purchase Order No: _____

Credit Card Payment:
☐ VISA
☐ MASTERCARD
☐ AMER EXP
☐ DISCOVER

Card Number: _____

Expiration Month and Year: _____

Card Holder Name: _____

Card Holder Signature: _____

Order Online: www.Scholarship-Workbook.com